She almost fainted when he turned and looked at her. He wore a dead expression. From the eyes down, the face was hideously slack, as though all the muscles of cheeks and mouth had been removed. The slack face seemed to hang from the eyes. And the eyes were dull, absorbing all light and reflecting none.

As he started toward her, smeared, stained and hideous, she turned and ran toward the door.

It was like one of the nightmares of childhood, like running through glue, your steps a slow drifting, while something comes after you, comes nearer.

JOHN D. MacDONALD

THE NEON JUNGLE

A FAWCETT GOLD MEDAL BOOK

Fawcett Publications, Inc., Greenwich, Conn.

Pre-1979

The Neighborhood

You can find people who will tell you about the neighborhood. Each will have his special vision. All those visions can never be added together, for perhaps, like a raddled and lusty woman reaching the weary end of middle age, the neighborhood has been all things to all men.

But there is still violence in her.

Ask that pair of college kids who came to sample the factory wenches last year, and broke their faces against stone Polack fists.

There is still money in her.

The numbers operators will tell you that. And those who get high rents for certain shabby houses near the Saegar Mill. And those Monday loan sharks, the six-for-five boys, who make a fine art of collection.

She is still colorful.

Down the narrow streets marches the neon. A fizzing and sputter and crackle of BAR GRILL LOUNGE INN and ROOMS APTS HOTEL and POOL BILLARDS BOWLING and TRIPLE FEATURE GIRLS BALLOOM CLUB FLOOR SHOW.

But here the feathers hang tired on the rumps of the floor-show ponies, and there is no self-conscious reading of Proust in satined dressing rooms. These are weary bitter-mouthed dollies, who take a percentage on the drinks you buy them.

The neon is green and red and blue, and there are always a few dead letters, though not usually as spectacular as the night the Essex Tavern lost its first two letters.

Do not think that the neighborhood is linked to downtown. It is a separate country, and there are many dingy unlighted streets between that minor neon jungle and the richer flavors of downtown.

And do not think that it is the abode, the stomping ground, of only the pimp, sharpie, and floozy set. There are the residential streets and they are narrow and poorly laid out, leading the visitor in infuriating circles. There are caste distinctions between the streets. There are churches and schools and many, many children.

There are gaunt bleak-faced textile mills, rumbling, clattering on the hot summer days, going abruptly silent at five to disgorge the slack-clad girls who make crow noises and clown with each other as they walk home into the narrow streets, passing the asphalted playgrounds of the schools they so recently attended, some of them already swelling with the fruit that will become a new shrillness on those same playgrounds.

There are empty mills with broken windows, like eyes that accuse.

Once upon a time it was all land that belonged to Abraham Townsend, and he and his eight strong sons farmed it well.

Later a grandson of Abraham started a general store, and that store became the nucleus of a village. There was another village two miles away, and they were of equal size. The new village was called, of course, Townsend, and it grew quickly. It became a gabled town of peasant houses. But the other village grew more quickly. Both of them, after the Civil War, became sprinkled with

Victorian horrors, all gingerbread and turrets. Then Townsend was absorbed, and it became a part of the city, and the name was lost, and it became simply the neighborhood.

It is all in the old ledgers down in City Hall.

Children grow up quickly in the neighborhood.

At night the lace-eared toms yell of love and passion in the narrow alleys, and the wagon picks up the broken-shoe bums from their newspaper nests. By day the sun bakes the narrow yards and not much wind gets in to stir the curtains, and milk sours quickly. A brave and wheelless Pierce Arrow sits window-deep in weeds in a vacant lot, and the rat-gnawed back seat is a place of juvenile assignation when dusk comes blue down the streets.

In the look of the narrow houses at night on the residential streets there is a flavor of violence. Not the sort of violence of the neon jungle, but a violence that is more quiet, and desperate.

It is a place of neighborhood stores and few chains. It is said that you can buy anything in the neighborhood. If you know where to look. Whom to see. When to see him.

When the hot weather starts, the police know that one of the quiet narrow houses will erupt. On the slow warm evenings a street will come alive to the screams of that final terror. And always the neighbors know which house it will be. They run out and they look toward the house. They sit a cautious time before the tentative investigation. Usually the screams stop quickly. There is something ultimate about the homely weapons of the quiet streets. A hammer, a hatchet, a butcher knife, a piece of pipe. They are decisive. After the violence there is the dumb weeping.

At night the only light in the Varaki Quality Market, a boxlike cinder-block structure, is the red neon around the clock. The family lives in the big shabby frame house adjoining the market. City houses stop on the nearby corner. A stranger to the neighborhood, anyone who had just moved onto the same block, for example, would perhaps not have sensed the drifting threat of violence that is like the trembling of the air before the first crash of thunder.

But the others had been there a long time. And so, on

that warm night, when the screaming started, they knew with neighborhood instinct precisely where to look. And the old women compressed their pale lips and nodded and nodded and waited silently for the end of the screaming. . . .

Chapter One

A CITY BUS hissed at the corner and was silent, then
snorted off through the milky dusk. She saw the light
pattern through the elm leaves and saw the bus was
headed downtown. Down where all the lights were. When
she had come here the elm branches had been naked raw.
And it had been harder then to stay in the small third-
floor room in the vast shabby frame house and think of
lights and people and movement and forgetting.

It was like the leaves growing to cover the city sounds,
the city lights. This slow change. The small room becoming more womb than prison. She sat Buddha fashion
on the straight hard chair near the window in the dusk
grayness, motionless. She sat in black corduroy slacks,
hands resting on the sharply flexed knees, head tilted a
bit so that the smoke from the cigarette in the corner
of her mouth made a thin upward line past the smooth
cheek and half-closed eyes. The cheap phonograph on
the floor beside the chair was turned so low that the
golden ovals of the horn sounds came faintly through
the needle hiss. The record ended and she took the cigarette from her mouth and leaned down and lifted the
arm and set it back at the beginning. The silken heavi-
ness of the dark copper hair swung forward and when
she straightened up she swung it back with a quickness
of her head.

She thought of them down there, working in the stark
white fluorescence, handling the late rush, and she
thought carefully of how it would be to go down there
now. She imagined just how it would be and she decided
she could do it now. Gus had seemed to know just how
the little man with the clown face had torn her apart,
had opened up the neatly mended places, finding the
fracture lines of old wounds. She had not broken in front
of the little man. Gus had stepped in angrily.

9

"Lieutenant, you know you talk to my daughter. You don't talk that way."

"Daughter-in-law, Pop. Where the hell did Henry find *her?*"

"Lieutenant, you go chase thiefs. Don't bother good people. Bonny, you go upstairs. Rest. You work a long time."

She had left quickly, precariously, not looking at the grotesque clown face, stepping out from behind the cash register and crossing the store and going through the side door, through the narrow shed and up the steps into the big kitchen, managing even to smile and bob her head at the monolithic Anna standing by the stove, and through the rooms packed solidly with the massive furniture, and up the two flights of stairs, and down the hall, and into her own room, shutting the door behind her without a sound, and taking the three steps to the bed and lying there, moving over a bit so her forehead could be pressed against the wall, against the faded paper pattern of blue flowers.

It is meant, she thought, that I shall be always rescued by the Varaki family. But they started rescuing me too late. They came after all the other things had been stamped on my face and in my eyes, the things the lieutenant saw so quickly and so easily, and so contemptuously.

It isn't true, she thought, that you go down like a rocket, like a dropped stone. It is, perhaps, more like a slow-motion picture of a bouncing ball. It starts, tritely enough, with a betrayal, with a heartbreak. It means so much then. Dev had meant too much back in the good years that were now like things on the other side of a wall. Dev with the Irish smile and the quick hands and the vanity. Dev, who did not like his hair mussed, and did not like to be touched, and at last was chased away by too much love, fearing that there was a stickiness in possession.

And so then, that first time, you let go and took the first long fast drop down to the absolute bottom. The first drop of the ball. At the bottom was death and the slow-falling ball touched it, felt the coldness and the hardness and rebounded, climbing back up—all the way, you thought. But not quite all the way. A time of being poised there, and then another drop. And another, so that the touch of death came more often, and became more familiar, and became less frightening. Then you could look up and see where you used to be. Each bounce was less. Each time there was less resilience.

Then deftly, miraculously, Henry Varaki had cushioned that last fall. She'd been in San Francisco then. The nights had been oddly merged, so that there seemed to be no days between them. She remembered being noisy in one place and being pushed out by someone whose face she tried to claw. Then, in the momentary sobriety of the drenching rain, the rain that caked her dress to her body, she thought they might phone the police, and that last thirty days had been a horror. She had run in the rain and fallen, and run some more. Then there was another place, and lights, and an alley fight between sailors, and more running. One high heel was gone and the running was a crooked, grotesque gallop. There was something hot and humming behind her eyes, something hot and roaring in her ears. She ran down a crooked street, tilted so that it swung her against the wall. . . .

Then there was a long time when everything was mixed up. Henry said later it was eleven days. It was like coming out of a long jumbled tunnel, full of noises and shoutings and crazy whistling lights, into a sudden calm place. She opened her eyes. A big-shouldered kid with a blond burr head in Army khaki with sergeant's stripes sat by the narrow window, his chair tilted back against the wall. It was very quiet. Beyond the window was fog. Beyond the fog was a muffled heavy bleat, metronomic, as though some great animal were caught out there. Traffic whispered through the fog with muslin horn sounds. It was a strange room and she did not want to turn her head, as that seemed too great an effort. She closed her eyes for just a moment, and when she opened them again the window was dark and the sergeant was not there. She turned her head a bit toward the source of light, and saw him sitting by the lamp, still reading.

He seemed to sense her stare. He put the book aside and came over to her and stood frighteningly huge beside the bed and laid the back of his hand against her forehead with a miraculous gentleness.

"What happened?" she asked weakly.

"You mean who shoved you, Bonny? A pneumonia bug. You didn't have any resistance."

"Who are you?" Her voice felt trembly.

"Henry Varaki. Don't try to ask questions. I'll see if I can cover it. I was just walking around with one of the guys. You were out like a light. A guy was holding you up against a wall and beating hell out of you. We took care of him quick and took you to a hospital. For some damn reason they wouldn't take you. You felt like you were burning up. My buddy had a friend who gave him the use of this place, so we brought you back here and rounded up a doctor. Malnutrition, alcoholism, pneumonia, anemia, and possible internal injuries from the beating you took. My, that doctor was real intrigued with you, Bonny. He said he could get you in a charity ward, but I couldn't swing any special nurses or anything, so I figured I could take care of you myself. My friend went on east. It's been . . . let me count, eleven days. You've had glucose and oxygen and all the antibiotics in the book, Bonny. The doc comes in every morning to check. You've been out of your head until day before yesterday. Since then you've been mostly sleeping. He said this morning you'd probably wake up clear as a bell today."

He sponged her face with gentleness. He held her head up and held a glass to her lips. She was far too weak to sit up alone, much less stand. He took care of her needs with a calm deftness that was so matter of fact that she felt neither shame nor shyness. In the morning, before the doctor was due, he gave her a sponge bath. She looked down and was shocked at her pale wasted body, at the shrunken breasts, the spindle legs, the hipbones that looked sharp enough to pierce the pallid skin.

The doctor came. He was a gruff, bustling man. He addressed most of his questions to Henry, a few to her. He wrote out two prescriptions and said, "You're a tough young woman. Keep this up and you'll come back fast. Henry, go out in the other room and close the door."

"Why, Doc?"

"Just do it, Henry."

Henry left the room and closed the door gently. The doctor looked at her. His expression changed, became harder. "You are not only tough. You are lucky. You owe your life to him. He is a rare young man. I don't know whether you can understand how rare. You people are always looking for angles. All you can do for him is get your strength back as fast as you can and get out of here. You'll be doing him a favor. When he was a kid I bet he kept birds with broken wings in boxes, with homemade splints. He didn't sleep for the first fifty hours you were here. He was on his way east. A thirty-day leave before shipping out. Don't try any of your sleek angles on him, young lady. You barely escaped burial, courtesy of the city of San Francisco. Don't try to say anything to me in explanation or apology. At this particular moment, I don't particularly want to hear the sound of your voice. I heard enough of what you said in delirium. So did Sergeant Varaki. It wasn't pretty. What made it particularly ugly was the very obvious fact that you started with education, background, decent breeding. Something was left out of you. Garden-variety guts, I'd imagine. Don't go back to your alley-catting until the Sergeant is over the horizon."

She shut her eyes. She heard the doctor leave and heard him talking to Henry in the next room. The tears scalded out through her closed lids. After a time she wiped them away with a corner of the sheet.

Henry came in, grinning. "He says he doesn't have to come back, Bonny. Congratulations. You can go in for a checkup after you're on your feet."

"That's good."

"Hey, don't go gloomy on me. My God, I'm glad to have have somebody to talk to. Somebody who makes sense, that is."

Slowly at first, and then more rapidly, she began to gain weight and strength. He bought her pajamas and a robe. She leaned weakly on him while she took the first tottering steps. One circuit of the room exhausted her.

"How about my room?" she asked. "How about my clothes?"

He flushed. "I got the address out of you one day when you weren't too bad. I went over there. She'd moved your stuff out of your room. You owed six bucks. I paid it and brought the stuff back here. I went through it. Maybe I shouldn't have. Your clothes were pretty sad, Bonny. I gave the works to the Salvation Army. I got your personal stuff in a little box. Papers and letters and some photographs and stuff like that."

Everything in the world in one small box. She closed her eyes. "Will you do something for me, Henry?"

"Sure."

"That's a silly-sounding question, will you do something for me, after . . . everything. Go through the box, Henry. Take out my Social Security card. Take out my birth certificate. Take out the photostat of my college record. Throw everything else away."

"Everything?"

"Please."

The next day he shamefacedly gave her an envelope. "All the things you wanted saved are in there. And I stuck in a few pictures. Your mother and father. I figured you ought to hang onto those too."

"They were killed in—"

"You talked about that a lot. I know about that. You better save the pictures. You have kids someday, they'd like to know what your people looked like."

"Kids someday."

"Don't say it like that, Bonny. Don't ever say it like that."

That was the day she sat on a stool in front of the kitchen sink of the apartment with a big towel around her shoulders while he washed her hair. It took four soapings, scrubbings, rinses to bring it back to life. And then, when it was dry and she brushed it, he admired the color of it, and in the midst of his admiration she saw him suddenly get the first increment of awareness of her. It was something she was well practiced in seeing. She was still slat thin, weighing less than a hundred pounds, and she was without make-up, and he had seen her body at its ugliest, and heard all the ugly bits of her history, and yet he could still have that sudden glow of interest and appreciation in his eyes. It made her want to cry.

She began to take over a small part of the cooking and cleaning on the twenty-second day of his thirty-day leave. On the bathroom scales she weighed an even one hundred. She was five-seven and considered her proper weight to be about one twenty-two or three. She had not weighed that much in over a year.

"I've got to have clothes to get out of here, Henry."

"I've been thinking about that. I'll have to buy them. You'll have to tell me about sizes."

"I'll give you the sizes. Get something cheap. Have you written it down for me? All the money you've spent so far? You can't have much left."

"I've got some. Doc took it easy on me." He flushed brightly. "And I'm only telling you this so you won't worry. Pop sent me two hundred bucks. I got it day before yesterday."

"You've got to go home, Henry. You've got to see them."

"There'll be time."

"There won't be time. You keep saying that. They'll never understand why you didn't go home. Never."

"They know me pretty well, Bonny. They know if I didn't go home, there's a damn good reason."

"There's no reason good enough."

He had talked a lot about his family. The Varaki clan. "There's us three kids. Me and Walter and Teena. Teena's the baby. High-school gal. Walter's older than I am. Dark coloring, like the old lady was. His wife is Doris. She gives old Walter a pretty hard time. She's a pinwheeler, that gal. Then Jana is Pop's second wife. He married her last year. It was like this. You see, Mom died three years ago. Some of Jana's relatives, farm people, sent her to stay with us so she could go to business school. She's two years younger than Walter, and two years older than me. Big husky farm girl. With her in the house, Anna, that's Pop's older sister, came to sort of keep house for us. Then Pop ups and marries Jana. It made the whole family sore as hell. Especially Doris. Anna stayed on. Pop and Jana are happy. Well, hell, it's a happy house. Great big old ruin of a place. The market used to be in the downstairs. Pop built a new market right next door right after the war. It's run like a supermarket. Mostly the people that work there live in the house too. There's three floors. Ten bedrooms. Always something going on. Usually something crazier than hell. Pop and his old cronies play card games in the kitchen and yell at each other in old-country talk. Everybody pitches in."

He had talked about them enough so that she felt as though she knew them. Knew them better than some of the dim-faced people of the last few years.

She wrote down the sizes, and he left her alone. He was back in two hours, burdened with boxes. There was a shiny inexpensive suitcase hooked over one big finger. The boxes towered almost to his eyes.

"You got too much, Henry!"

"Come on Bonny. Start opening. It's like Christmas, hey?"

"Too much."

He seemed to have an intuitive understanding of color, of what she could and couldn't wear with that dark copper hair. Yet he had bought the sort of clothes she hadn't worn in a long time. Nubby tweed skirts, soft pale sweaters.

"I hope you like this kind of stuff," he said nervously. "There was one picture of you in all that stuff. That stuff I threw out. You were in this kind of thing and I sort of liked it."

There were two skirts, three sweaters, two blouses, three sets of nylon panties and bras, two pairs of shoes, one with two-inch wedge heels and one pair of sandals with ankle straps. She went into the bedroom and put on one outfit. She looked at herself in the mirror, looking first at the fit and length and then suddenly noticing her own flushed face, eager eyes, half-smile. The smile faded away. She bit her lip. Her gray eyes looked enormous in the too thin face. She went back out to him.

"Bonny, you look swell! You look wonderful!"

"I don't know how . . . I don't know how to . . ."

He handed her a small box. "I picked up some junk jewelry. Dime-store stuff. A kind of a clip thing and a bracelet. I thought . . ."

She sat and heard him come over, felt his hand warm and steady on her shoulder. "Look, I didn't want for it to make you cry. Hell, Bonny. I didn't mean it to work like this. Please, honey."

He went out again in the late afternoon to buy groceries for their dinner. She packed her things in the bag. She wrote a note.

"Thanks for everything, Henry. I've got your home address. I'll send the money there when I get it. You've been swell. Now you've got time to hurry home and see them and get back before your leave is over." She signed it and read it over. It would have to do. There weren't any right words to tell him. The doctor had told her what she had to do. And the doctor had been very, very right.

Her legs felt odd and stilty as she went down the two flights of stairs and out onto the street. The sunshine looked too bright. Her feet looked and felt far away.

She walked down the block and the shiny new suitcase cut into her hand. It was light and there was very little in it. The blocks were very long. People and traffic moved too fast. She heard the hard slap of leather against the sidewalk and she turned and saw him and she tried to run. He caught her and held her with his big hands tight above her elbows, hurting her. There were odd patches of white on his face and his blue eyes were so narrow they were nearly closed.

"What are you doing?"

"Let me go. Let me go."

He took her back, one hand still folded tightly around her thin arm, the suitcase in his other hand. She walked with her head bowed. At the foot of the stairs he picked her up lightly in his arms and carried her up. She was crying then. Crying with her face turned against the side of his strong young throat.

He got the door open and kicked it shut behind them. He dropped the suitcase, paused with her still in his arms and read the note, and then walked to the big chair in the living room and sat down with her, holding her, letting her cry the tears of weakness and frustration.

It was a long time before she was able to stop.

"Where would you have gone?"

"It doesn't matter."

"It does matter."

"No."

"It has to matter to you or you'd have been better off if that drunk had killed you."

"I would have been better off."

"Self-pity. For God's sake, sometimes you make me sick."

"I make myself sick."

"Oh, shut up! The doctor said to throw you out the minute you could walk. Fine! What does that make me? A sucker who wasted his leave. Something has to come of it. Something more than that."

They stayed there until the last of the dusk was gone and the room was dark. Darkness gave her a certain courage. She said, "What happens does seem to matter more than . . . it did before. I don't know why it should. All this has been like . . . being born again. Being cared for like a baby. Fed, bathed, taught to walk. I could almost come back to life."

He kissed her lightly and stood up and set her on her feet. It was the first time he had kissed her. He said, "It was good to hear you say that, Bonny."

He turned on the lights. They squinted in the brightness and smiled uncertainly at each other, and talked in small casual voices through dinner and through the short evening until she went to bed after helping him make up his bed on the studio couch in the small living room.

Chapter Two

THE NEXT MORNING Henry was moody and thoughtful. He spent a lot of time standing at the windows, looking down at the street. He jingled change in his pockets. He paced restlessly.

After lunch he got up and brought more coffee from the stove and filled their cups. He sat down opposite her.

"I've got seven more days furlough, Bonny."

"I know. You said you could hitch a plane ride. Why don't you, Henry? I'll stay right here. Honestly. Then you could come back here, and by then I should be strong enough. I could get a job, maybe."

"I'm not going home. I don't want to hear any more about it."

"Goodness! Don't snarl."

"I've got something figured out."

"What do you mean?"

"I told you it's a big house. There's room. God knows there's plenty of work, so it wouldn't be like you were sponging on the old man. He drives everybody. Then you'd be getting the allotment money. It wouldn't be much."

She stared at him. "Allotment?"

"I can't leave you this way. I got to know that you're set. And I know enough about you to know that you won't be set unless you got a reason. And the only reason that's going to mean anything to you is to have somebody depending on you and trusting you. I can get a cab and we can go fill out the forms and get the blood tests or whatever you have to have in California. And then, by God, you'll be a Varaki, and you'll have the whole damn family on your side. The way I figure it, it will be an arrangement. I haven't written the family any of this. They won't know a damn thing, except you're my wife. And that'll be all they need to know."

She rested her hands flat on the table and shut her eyes for long seconds. "What are you, Henry? Twenty-three?"

"Twenty-two."

"I'm a twenty-six-year-old tramp."

"Don't talk like that!"

"A tramp. A semi-alcoholic. A girl who works the bars and works the men she finds in the bars. A girl who . . . can't even remember all their faces. It's good luck instead of good judgment that I'm not diseased. Bonita Wade Fletcher. A great little old gal. I've been tossed in the can twice here and once in L.A. That's what you're trying to wish on your family, Henry. On decent people."

"My God, you like to wallow in it, don't you?"

"You're playing a part now, Henry. A big fat dramatic part. Saving the fallen. Rescuing the scarlet woman. My God, look at me!"

"I'm looking."

"I walk a certain way and talk a certain way and look at men a certain way, and your whole damn family would have to be blind not to see it. I'm just one big smell of stale bedroom and warm gin. No, Henry. Not on your life."

"I say you got to look at yourself and understand that you got to have some kind of a reason to prop you up. You forgot how to stand up by yourself."

"Love. Love goes with marriage. I couldn't love you. I haven't got enough love left for anybody. I gave it all away. Free samples."

"I haven't said a damn word about love. This is just an arrangement. Goddamn it, you go back there to Johnston as Mrs. Henry Varaki and let the name prop you up until you can stand by yourself. Or maybe you don't go for Varaki. Too foreign, maybe. Low class."

"No. No."

"I go away and I come back. O.K. By then you know. Either way we break it up legal. And to hell with you if you let me down."

"You said it's a nice business. Profitable. How do you know I won't stay tied around your neck, lushing on your father's profits from the store for the rest of your life?"

His voice softened. "Bonny, I listened to you for a lot of days and nights. I listened to a lot of things. I know more about you than you know about yourself."

She put her head down on her wrist on the table. She rocked her head from side to side. "No," she said in a broken voice. "No. No. No."

It lasted until midnight. She felt utterly drained and exhausted. She felt as though she had no more will or identity of her own, as if some great force had picked her up and carried her along. She was sick with the strain, with the long bitter hours of it.

"All right," she heard herself say. "All right then, Henry."

He looked at her for a long time and then grinned. "We Varakis got a reputation for stubbornness."

They went down in a taxi at ten the next morning. They filled out the application forms, had blood tests made, were told when to reappear for the license and civil ceremony. There was a great deal of constraint between them. That evening she straightened up after making up the studio couch for him and said in a deadly flat tone of voice, "You can start sleeping with me if you want to. You ought to get that much, at least, but I won't blame you if you refuse the kind offer, because it isn't exactly what you might call a generous offer. It's more like maybe offering somebody a cigarette. The last one in the pack. The kind that are all . . ."

"Shut up and go to bed, for God's sake."

"Just drop in any time. I won't consider it an inconvenience."

"Will you shut up? Or will I shut you up?"

"Oh, goody! We're engaged! We're engaged!"

"Good night, Bonny."

"Good night, Henry."

They were married on a cold rainy Thursday in late November at five minutes of noon. They taxied back to the apartment in rigid uncomfortable silence. My happy wedding day, she thought.

Henry said he'd be back in a while and he went out. She sat and watched the rain run down the window. My wedding day. The bride carried a bouquet of raspberry blossoms. Henry came back in an hour, his clothes rain-spattered. He carried a bundle into the kitchen. He came back in and tossed a flat box onto her lap. "I put champagne on ice."

"Dandy. One sip and I'll go on a nine-week bat."

He sat and looked gravely at her. "Why do you do it to yourself, Bonny?"

"Do what, husband darling?" she asked blandly. "What have we here in the box, husband darling?"

"Open it and find out."

"Oh, goody! A present for your winsome little wife, perhaps."

She took off the paper and opened the box. She looked at what it contained. She heard the rain. She knew she should look over at him. She could not quite force herself to look at him. My wedding day, I forgot that it was his, too. Selfish, self-pitying nag. She took it out of the box. The lace on the bodice of the nightgown was like white foam. She looked at it for a moment and then buried her face in it. A great raw sob hurt her throat.

He came to her and held her. When she could speak she said, "What are you ... trying to do to me?"

"Keep you from doing too much to yourself, Bonny. I know it isn't a marriage like in the movies. Is there any law about having as much as we can, even if it isn't perfect?"

"Nothing has ever been more perfect for me. I've acted foul to you. I'm terribly, desperately sorry, Henry. So damn sorry."

"You'll wear it?"

"Of course."

Later she was able to laugh in a way in which she had not laughed in years. It was a good gayness. Later, in the darkened bedroom, she felt oddly virginal. She had to push the bitter, ironic thoughts back out of her mind. His big hands were tender and gentle, and there was a warm strength to him. Gentleness stirred her as fierceness never could. She felt strangely shy, almost demure. It was all sweet and moving, and he did not find out until afterward, when he kissed her eyes, that she wept.

"Why, darling?" he whispered.

And she could not tell him the truth. That she wept because she regretted the years that had left her so little to give him, and had turned her own responses into nothingness. He was big and gentle. A nice kid. She could feel that, and nothing more, no matter how she tried.

"Why are you crying?" he repeated.

"Because I think I love you, my darling," she lied. And

she knew that her lie was a strong fence that would be around her during the time he would be gone.

The day he left he gave her the bus ticket and twenty dollars. He said he'd change the insurance and make out the allotment forms. He kissed her hard. She watched his broad back as he walked off. He did not turn again.

She was on the bus two hours later. The wire from Henry's father, Gus Varaki, had said, TELL HER THIS IS WHERE SHE LIVES NO NONSENSE.

It was a long bus trip. Nights and darkness and flashing lights and muted sleep sounds around her. Early-morning stops at the wayside stations. The grainy, sticky, heavy feeling of sleeping in a tilted seat. She wanted to feel that the blue and silver bus was taking her out of one life and into a new one. But you could not empty yourself of everything, become a shell to be refilled. Wherever you went, you had to take yourself, take all your own corrosive juices and splintered memories and patterned reactions. Henry became unreal after the first day of travel. He was a gentle hand that touched her forehead, seeking the dry heat of fever. A big muscular kid who walked lightly. A faceless kid. A kid who joined the ranks of all the other faceless ones. His eyes had been blue, his hair coarse, blond, bristly. Mrs. Henry Varaki.

Gus and Jana met her at the grubby bus station in Johnston. By then she was too weary to look for their reactions. She knew only that Gus Varaki was a thick-bodied stocky man who hugged her warmly, and Jana was a plain sturdy girl who kissed her. They took her to a car and drove her through the afternoon streets, through snow that melted as it fell. They took her to a big house and to this third-floor room. Jana brought food. She went to sleep after a hot bath. She did not awaken until dusk of the following day.

It had taken her months to build confidence. Gus and Jana and Anna and Teena had helped. Walter seemed to have no reaction to her. His thin dark bitter pregnant wife, Doris, was actively unpleasant.

It had taken a long time to rebuild. In March it was all torn down again when the wire came about Henry. The letter from his commanding officer came a week later, to the gloomy, depressed household.

Gus came to her room and sat stolidly, tears marking the unchanging gray stone of his face.

She told him twice that she was going to leave before he seemed to hear her. Then he looked at her slowly.

"Leave us, Bonny? No. You stay."

"I'm no help to you. I'm no good here."

"We want you. What other thing I can say?"

Jana later showed her the letter Henry had written his father. "I think I'll be O.K., Pop, but in a deal like this you can't be 100 per cent sure. If anything happens, make Bonny stay with you. Don't let her leave. She hasn't got any place to go. Keep her there until it looks like she can make out O.K. on her own."

Jana said, "That isn't why Gus wants you to stay, Bonny. Not on account of this letter. It's more than that. To him, you're like a part of Henry. The only part left. We . . . all want you."

"But you don't know. You don't know what I was when Henry came along and . . ."

Jana, sitting close, gently touched Bonny's lips with her fingertips. "Shush, Bonny."

"But I want you to know all of it."

"Why? To punish yourself, maybe? We weren't blind. We've watched you change. You aren't what you were."

And she had stayed, and it was June, and she had learned to take a pride in the quickness with which she could handle the big cash register at the check-out counter. She rarely had to examine the packaged goods to find the price. The regular customers knew her, and she talked with them. The first burden of grief had lifted from the big house. Gus Varaki had not recovered from it completely, and it did not seem that he would. Some of the life had gone out of him. Bonny remembered the way it had been when she had first come there, finding Gus and his young bride standing close in corners, laughing together in a young way, blushing and moving apart when someone noticed them. There was no longer the busty, impulsive caress, a hard pinch of waist, a growl and nibble at the firm young throat. The loss of his son had in some odd way placed Jana in the role of daughter rather than young wife. And Jana no longer would watch her husband across the room in the evening after the store closed, and grow heavy-lidded, soft-mouthed, to at last go up the stairs with him, saying good night to the others in a faraway voice.

Jana was the sort of girl who, at first glance, was quite

plain. Face a bit broad, pale skin, shiny nose, hair that was not quite brown and not quite blonde and very fine-textured, body that was solidly built, eyes that were pale and not quite blue and not quite gray.

But at third glance, or fourth, you began to notice the glow of health, a silky, glowing ripeness. Her waist and ankles and wrists were slim, and she moved lightly and quickly. You saw the soft natural wave in her hair, and you sensed the sweetness of her, the young animal cleanliness, and you saw then the softness and clever configuration of the underlip, the high roundness of breast.

She had no cleverness or mental quickness. Routine tasks suited her best, and she could not seem to acquire enough speed on check-out. She could handle heavy sacks and crates with lithe ease. She ate as much as any man. And she had a good true warm instinct about people. She was a good wife for Gus. Yet Bonny guessed from the puzzlement she often saw in Jana's eyes, from her frequent fits of irritability, that she was not being treated as a wife. She was receiving the affection of a daughter. And Gus walked heavily and did not smile much.

Today the man with the clown face had come in. Lieutenant Rowell. A thick-legged, fat-bellied little balding man with thin narrow shoulders, and a face that made you want to laugh. Button nose, owl eyes, a big crooked mouth. His forehead bulged and it gave his face a look that was not exactly the look of an infant, but rather something prenatal, something fetal.

He was from the local precinct. The area was one in which there were factories, alleys, down-at-the-heels rooming houses, poolrooms, juvenile gangs, tiny shabby public parks, candy stores with punchboards, brick schoolyards. There were long rows of identical houses. There was always trouble in the neighborhood. Rowell was, they said, a good cop for the neighborhood, inquisitive, bullying, cynical, and merciless. He had watched Bonny other times he had been in.

Today he had said, without warning, and in a voice that stopped all other talk and motion in the store, "I like to know everybody I got in the neighborhood, Bonny. Everybody that moves in. It saves time. I got to get a transcript of the application for license to find out the name you used to run under. Fletcher, they tell me. So I check it through on the teletype. Just routine."

She could not look at him or speak.

"What's on the books out there is between you and me, honey. All I say is this: stay off my streets at night. Stay out of my joints."

In the silence she heard Pop chunk the cleaver deeply into the chopping block. He came out around the end of the long meat counter, saying, "Lieutenant, you know you talk to my daughter."

You build carefully, and something behind that clown face can tear it all down. His streets. His joints. Some people from the neighborhood had been in there. It would spread fast. Walter Varaki had been on one knee in an aisle, marking cans and stacking them on a low shelf. Rick Stussen, the fat blond butcher, had been behind the meat counter with Gus, running the slicer.

She sat in the small third-floor room by the gabled window, and knew it was time to go back down. To wait longer would make it more difficult. The record was finished again. She lifted the arm back and placed it at rest and turned the switch. The turntable stopped. It had been a gift from Gus and Jana at Christmas. Another bus hissed at the corner. It was headed downtown. Down to where the lights were, down to places of quick forgetting. There was a tide that ran strongly, and for a time she had been in an eddy near a lee shore, caught in a purposeless circling. One gentle push and the tide would catch her again and take her on, away from this quietness, away from these people who trusted her merely because one of them had married her.

She got up from the chair and stretched the stiffness out of her long legs, cramped from sitting so long in one position. She went down the hall to the third-floor bathroom, turned on the light, and examined her face in the mirror. She looked at herself and saw what Rowell had seen. A guilty furtiveness in the gray eyes. The cast of weakness across the mouth, with its sullen swollen lips. The look of the chippy. Chippy in a white cardigan, in black corduroy slacks. She made an ugly face at herself, dug lipstick out of the pocket of the slacks, and painted on a bold mouth, bolder than the mouth she had worn these last months.

She went down and found Jana swamped at the checkout, five people waiting with loaded baskets. Jana gave her a strained smile and moved gratefully over. They worked together, unloading the baskets onto the counter. Bonny's fingers were staccato on the register keys, while Jana packed the groceries in bags and cartons. Bonny was curt and unsmiling with the customers.

Soon there was no one waiting. She straightened the stacks of bills in the register drawer, took the machine total for the day, and, using the register as an adding machine, quickly totaled the checks that had been taken in.

Gus came over, wiping his hands on his apron, saying too cheerfully, "You don't get upset about him with the funny face."

"It's all right."

"Let's see a smile."

"It's all right," she said, unsmiling. Another customer wheeled a loaded basket up. Gus walked away. Bonny worked the keys so hard that her fingers stung.

Chapter Three

PAUL DARMOND finished his pencil draft of his bi-monthly report to the Parole Board and tossed the yellow pencil onto the rickety card table. In the morning he'd take it down to his small office in the county courthouse and get one of the girls in Welfare to type it up. At least there'd be no kickbacks on this report. No skips. No incidents. He stood up and stretched and scuffed at his head with his knuckles. He was a tall lean man with a tired young-old face, a slow way of moving. He felt the empty cigarette pack and crumpled it and tossed it into the littered fireplace.

It was nine o'clock and he felt both tired and restless. He had been so intent on the report that an unconscious warm awareness of Betty had crept into the back of his mind. That awareness had changed his environment back to the apartment, that other apartment of over a year ago. And when he had finished the report and looked up, there had been a physical shock in the readjustment.

It's funny, he thought, the way it keeps happening to you. Relax for a few minutes, and she sneaks back into your life. And it's like it never happened—the sudden midnight convulsions, the frantic phone calls, the clang-ing ambulance ride, Dr. Weidemann walking slowly into the waiting room, mask pulled down, peeling the rubber gloves from his small clever hands.

"I'm sorry, Paul. Damn sorry. Pregnancy put an extra load on her kidneys. There was some functional weak-ness there we didn't catch. They quit completely. Poi-soned her. Blood pressure went sky high. Her heart quit, Paul. She's dead. I'm damn sorry, Paul."

But the mind kept playing that same vicious trick of bringing her back, as though nothing had happened, as though she sat over there in the corner of the room, reading, while he finished his report.

Then she would say in her mocking way, in which there was no malice. "Have all your little people been good this time, darling?"

"Like gold."

She understood how it was. She had understood how a graduate sociologist working on his doctorate could take this poorly paid job just to gain field experience in his major area of interest, and then find himself cleverly trapped by that very interest, trapped by the people who were depending on him to fight for them. It had been a rather wry joke between them.

"I don't mind, Paul," she had said. "I honestly don't. Please don't worry about it. We can manage. We'll always manage."

"The pay will be spread pretty thin after you have the kid."

"We'll put him to work and make him pay for the next one."

"That's easy to say."

"Stop it, Paul. You love what you're doing. You're rebuilding lives. That's worth a little scrimping and pinching."

"I could teach at the university and make more than this, for God's sake."

Now, of course, the pay didn't make much difference. It went for rent for the one-room apartment down in the neighborhood where most of his parolees were, for hasty meals at odd hours, for gas for the battered coupe. There was nothing left now but the work.

He decided to walk down to the corner for some cigarettes. As he was going down the front steps a police car pulled up in front, on the wrong side of the street, and Rowell stuck his clown face out the window. "How you doing, Preacher Paul?"

Paul felt the familiar regret and anger that always nagged at him when one of his people slipped. He went over to the car. "Who is it, Rowell?"

"You mean you think it's possible for one of those little darlings of yours to go off the tracks? And them all looking so holy."

"Have your fun. Then tell me."

Rowell's tone hardened. "My fun, Darmond? You give me a lot of fun with those jokers of yours."

"If you'd get off their backs, they'd make it easier."

"If I get off their backs they'll walk off with the whole district."

Paul knew that it was an old pointless argument. Nothing could change Rowell. Paul had followed closely the results of the experimental plastic surgery performed on habitual criminals to determine the effect of physiogmony on criminal behavior. He suspected that Andrew Rowell had, throughout adolescence, suffered the tortures of hell because of his ludicrous face. It had made him a vicious, deadly fighter. At some point in adolescence the road had forked, and Rowell had taken the path that made him a successful police officer, rather then the criminal he could have been. Once when they had both been relaxed after discussing a particular case, Paul had tried to explain his theory to Andy Rowell. He knew he would never forget how white the man's face had turned, how clear was the look of murder in those owl eyes.

Rowell had said then, in a labored rusty voice, "There are two kinds of people. The hell with all your theories. Just two kinds, Preacher. The straight and the crooked. The straight ones don't go bad. The bad ones can pretend to go straight. They can fool you. But they don't ever kid me. Ever."

And Paul had asked gently, "I suppose you think they're born crooked?"

"I know they are. And I can spot 'em on the street. I can smell 'em. All the way from the punks to the big dealers."

"What do you want to talk to me about?" Paul asked gently now, forgetting his own anger, remembering how astonishingly sensitive and helpful Rowell had been after Betty's death.

"I want to talk about that Varaki outfit."

"Here? Or do you want to come in? I was on my way down to the corner to get cigarettes."

"Hop in. I'll drive you down."

Paul walked around the car and got in. Rowell parked on the corner and he went in and came back with cigarettes and got in beside him. Rowell drove back to the house and turned off the motor and turned in the seat, one arm along the seat back.

"We can talk here. O.K., Preach."

"Go ahead."

"I don't like the setup. You shilled Pop Varaki into taking on that punk who makes deliveries for him. Lockter."

"Vern Lockter is a good kid. He had some trouble. He hasn't been in trouble for two years. He doesn't have to report to me any more. Pop says he's a good worker."

"When he isn't working he dresses pretty sharp, Preach."

"So what? He lives there, eats there. So he saves his money and spends it on clothes."

"He wears his sharp clothes to bowling alleys, the fights, the beer joints. He knows all the local sharpies."

"But he hadn't been in trouble for over two years."

"O.K., O.K. We'll drop him for a minute. I understand you're wishing off another punk on Pop Varaki."

"That's right. I went to bat. Gus needs a new kid around. There are more orders to deliver. Vern Lockter can't do the odd jobs around the place. There's just Gus and Stussen and Walter Varak and Vern. So this kid is coming down from the industrial school. His name is Jimmy Dover."

"I know his name. I know the record. He lived with an aunt. He and two of his pals lifted a heap and busted into a gas station. They got caught and one of his friends made a break and got shot through the head and this Dover was carrying a switch-blade knife when they brought him in. Juvenile Court put him in the school. He did two years. He's eighteen. While he was up there, the aunt disappeared. They couldn't trace her. What kind of a hold you got over Gus, anyway?"

"He's a good man, that's all. And Jimmy is O.K. I talked it over with him a month ago. I drove Gus up and we both talked to him. Old Gus likes to help straighten a kid out."

"O.K. Lockter and Dover. That makes two of them. And the redhead makes three."

"What do you mean?" Paul asked sharply.

"Just what I say. I can smell 'em. So I checked back on her. San Francisco police. Twice they rapped her on a D and D. Henry must have inherited it from his old man. He must have had reformer blood, like you got, Preach."

"I suppose you went over and let her know about it?" Paul said softly.

"It keeps them in line if they know you know the score. Sure I did. She couldn't look me in the eye. Pop sent her into the house and raised hell with me."

"You've got a hell of a lot of tact. Don't you understand she's Gus's daughter-in-law?"

"I'm doing Gus a favor, for God's sake. I still haven't got to what's on my mind. You got the Fletcher girl, Dover, and Lockter. You got' em all living in that barn of a place with Stussen and the Varaki family. The three of them are going to get their heads together and figure some way of making a dime. Maybe they'll take it off the Varaki family. I wish they would. It would cure Gus of being noble. Maybe they'll try it some other way. When they do, it's my business. I'm letting you know, I don't like the setup, and I'm letting you know that I'm going to lean on all of them."

"Until they *do* make some kind of slip. Until you pressure them into it."

"Don't get hot, Preach. They all slip. I'm keeping my area clean. But it's getting tougher all the time. Somebody is pushing horse and tea again. Headquarters is riding me, and so is the Man. I just don't want any new kind of trouble on top of what I got already. And I'm damn sick of you feeding new ones into my back yard."

"I want you to do me a favor. Don't lean on Jimmy until he's had a chance to get his feet on the ground."

"I'll give him a week."

"That's big of you, Andy. Very generous."

"Sure. I remember Lerritti and Mendez and Conlon."

"Three, Andy, out of how many in the last four years? Eighty? Ninety?"

"Three so far. Isn't that what you mean?"

"Someday you'll see what I mean, Andy."

"I'm too stupid. I haven't had the education. I'm just a cop, Preacher."

Paul got out. "Good night. Andy."

"Two will get you five there'll be a capias out on this Dover in six months. And the next one won't go through Juvenile Court."

Rowell drove away. Paul stood and watched the taillights turn the next corner at cruising speed. He knew that Lieutenant Andy Rowell would cruise his district until it began to quiet down at two or three in the morning. He would sleep a few hours and be back at the precinct early in the morning. He had no life aside from the force. He drove his men and drove himself. Several times he had been in trouble because of too much damage inflicted on someone who "resisted arrest," but it had blown over. It was admitted that he ran the toughest area of a rough, gutty industrial city, and kept it as clean as any man could who had to work with a force on which there were too many political appointees, too many cousins of cousins. Through the night hours he would roam the district like a tough, homeless little bull terrier, showing his clown face in the rough joints, grimly amused at the silence that would last until he left. Once three citizens decided to prove to Rowell that it was bad practice to roam around the area alone. They whispered him into an alley mouth and worked him over. He pretended unconsciousness until he had a chance to wrench his right arm free. They had taken his detective special from its holster and tossed it back down the alley but the sap was in his right hip pocket, the thong dangling. Half blind with his own blood, dazed by the blows, he had instinctively hit the right one first. He left one dead in the alley. An ambulance took a second one. The third one was relatively unharmed. Rowell took him in, booked him, threw him in a cell, and then went himself to the hospital to have his gashed face stitched, his broken left wrist set. He put himself back on duty the next night, and methodically visited every dive in his district, with a hard gay grin on his bandaged clown face. He made his men travel in pairs. He always went alone.

Paul stood in the night long after the prowl car was out of sight. Two young girls came by, arm in arm, whispering and giggling. Red neon winked in the next block. Two soldiers stood on the corner, scuffling and laughing. A new convertible, glinting in the street light, cruised slowly down the narrow street, and there was a girl in it, singing nasally, sitting between two men. Paul felt the odd restlessness that had been gnawing at him for the past few months. An odd feeling that life was moving on to some bright, gay place, while he stood and watched it go by.

He went up the steps and through the unlocked door and turned left into his small ground-floor-front apartment with its old-fashioned bay windows, golden oak window seat, tan lace curtains, dark walls, dull furniture.

He thought about Vern Lockter. To Rowell, he had sounded more confident than he had felt. Lockter was a tall, powerful young man with a long narrow head, a quick flashing smile. He had an air of shrewd intelligence. Paul had the feeling that he had never got close to Vern Lockter. Lockter had said, almost too often, the usual things. Learned my lesson. Crime is for suckers. Look any man in the eye. And he had a habit of looking you so directly in the eye that it seemed contrived. There was an essential coldness about him. It had bothered Paul often enough for him to go and look Vern up. Vern, in work clothes, making up the orders, loading the truck, sweeping the store, had given Paul the strong impression that this was a part he was playing. Yet there was nothing you could put your finger on. The Varakis seemed to like him well enough, yet there was that same constraint that he had noticed in himself. Paul knew that the criminal for which there is no hope is the psychopathic personality, the man or woman born without the ability to give an emotional evaluation to right and wrong. To them there is only an intellectual distinction, and thus any violent act is permissible provided there is little or no chance of punishment. They are usually brighter than the norm, with a more pleasing personality. Just underneath the shell of personality, barely out of sight, is the cruel, unthinking violence of an animal.

He had been suspicious of Vern Lockter ever since their first meeting. His prison record had been excellent, as are the prison records of most psychopaths. Paul sensed his own inability to penetrate the mask of personality. He could not help thinking that Lockter was playing a part. And it did not seem logical that Lockter could be contented, over so long a period, to deliver grocery orders all over the city in the battered panel delivery truck with the faded letters on the side that spelled out Varaki's Quality Market. Though a lot of Gus's trade was local neighborhood customers, he carried fine meats and fancy gorceries and had, over the years, built up a large delivery trade, on both a cash and a credit basis.

And Lockter had been imprisoned for aggravated assault.

Paul slipped his report in a Manila envelope. He folded up the card table and prepared for bed. Somebody was playing a radio too loudly. Neon winked faintly against the tan lace curtains. He decided he would try to see Mrs. Henry Varaki on Monday when he went to the store with Jimmy Dover. He remembered seeing her. A tallish girl, quite pretty, with a quiet voice and a sulky mouth.

Chapter Four

WALTER VARAKI LAY on the bed with the pillows bunched under his head. The bed lamp made a bright light on the book he was reading. He had a cigar in the exact center of his mouth. He was vaguely conscious of Doris moving about the room, preparing for bed. It was the second time he had read the book. He was reading faster than usual, so he would get to the place where Mike Hammer takes the big blonde up to his apartment. That Hammer! There was a guy knew how to live. They didn't mess with him. Not twice, anyway. He had what it took with the women. He wasn't stuck in any two-bit grocery business.

"You know those damn cigars make me sick. I told you enough times. They make me sick!"

He took the cigar butt slowly from his lips and turned his head and gave her a look, the way Mike Hammer would have looked at her.

"That's a damn shame," he said, making his voice gravelly.

"A lot you care."

"Look, you're sleeping in the next room because you want more room in the bed now. Why don't you move your clothes in there and let me alone?"

"You know I don't feel good, and you got to try to make me sick with those stinking cigars. Everything around here smells like food or cigars."

He looked at the cigar. It had gone out of its own accord. He put it carefully in the glass ash tray. "It's out."

"Thank you so much," Doris said viciously.

"Boy, you have a happy disposition."

"Would you be happy, looking like this?"

She looked as if she were going to have the baby in the next ten minutes, but according to the doc it was still nearly a month off. That was a lot of yak about pregnancy making them bloom. Her black hair was stringy and sticky-looking and her complexion was all over pimples. He looked at her and wondered how the hell he's ever been able to think he was in love with her. Talk about her being sick. It turned his stomach to look at her. She'd always had a sharp tongue. These days she couldn't say anything pleasant to anybody. Sat around all day feeling sorry for herself.

"There's another jailbird coming on Monday," she said.

He turned back to his book. "Yeah."

"I told you to tell him not to have any more of them coming here. I got to raise a kid in this house. It looks like I'm going to spend the rest of my life raising kids in this crummy old house. I should have known you were giving me a big line with all that talk of getting out of here and going in some other line of work. You'll never get out. And I'll never get out. The least you can do is keep him from filling the place up with crooks and tramps. I don't want that Bonny touching my baby."

"Settle down, for God's sake they'll hear you all the way downstairs."

"I don't give a damn if they do. Nobody ever asks me for my opinion about anything around here."

"They don't have to ask you, baby."

"You didn't ever have that Vern Lockter looking at you the way he looked at me that day."

"You come prancing down the hall half naked, what you expect?"

"You just don't give a damn, do you?"

"Doris, for God's sake!"

"Go ahead. Curse at me. The old man won't let you go. You're the only son he's got left. One son and a man-crazy kid staying out half the night all the time. He won't let you go. Not him. He'll never pay us enough money so you can save enough to get out of here. We're both stuck. We might as well face it."

"Why don't you go to bed?"

"So you can enjoy your book. So you don't have to listen to me. So you don't have to pretend . . . Oh, hell!"

"Good night, for God's sake! Good night!"

She stared at him, then snatched her pajamas from the back of the closet door and went into the adjoining room and slammed the door. He gave a long sigh of relief and tried to get back into the book. But he needed a few minutes to quiet down. He tossed it aside and relit the cigar end, sucked the smoke deep into his lungs.

It seemed like there was a plot against him, the way everything worked out. God knew he'd never wanted to work in the store. Take Henry. He'd loved it. It was funny to think of never seeing Henry again. Way back there somewhere were the good days, when Mom had been around, when the store had been in the downstairs part of the house, when Teena had been too little to walk. Back when he and Henry had made raids on the store, with Pop and the help cussing them out.

No, he'd never wanted to work in the store. He'd taken those business courses in high school so he'd be able to get away from the grocery business. Everything seemed to go to hell for you when you weren't looking. Twenty-seven already, with twenty-eight coming up too soon. Too damn soon. Doris had raised a lot of hell when he'd given up four years' seniority at the post office to come back here and help out while Henry was in the Army. Now Henry was gone for keeps and it looked like he was stuck forever. And it looked like Doris would go on nagging for the rest of her life. Having the kid just made it worst, made it more impossible to get away.

He thought of her in the next room, lying heavily in the bed, and it was hard to think that she was the same Doris of way back when. He remembered that he first started watching her in typing class that next to last year of high. She sat diagonally ahead of him. Doris Antonelli. All the little things about her made his heart go fast. The way she sat so straight, and the way the yellow pencil looked shoved into her black hair, and the way her eyes were so quick, and the trick she had of flicking at her lower lip with the very tip of her tongue.

They'd started talking in the halls first, and it was a long time before she'd go out with him. Her people were real strict with her. They lived way the hell and gone out, and he remembered how it was, the incredible shocking softness of her lips that winter night inside that storm-door arrangement on her front porch, and then missing the late bus and walking all the way back through the snow, not even minding the cold, thinking of how she had felt in his arms.

The next year was the last year for both of them, and

they dated three and four nights a week, sometimes the movies, sometimes just walking together, sometimes just sitting in her living room until her old man would stick his head out of the kitchen and clear his throat a couple of times and he had to leave. Funny how, now, he remembered that they had talked and talked and talked, but now he couldn't remember what it was they talked about. Maybe they should have saved some of that talk until after marriage. It would have given them something to do.

He hadn't been thinking of marriage then. He'd been wanting to have her without that. And the way she acted, he thought he could, but somehow there didn't ever seem to be the right place or time. Without seeming to think about it or try, she always managed it so they weren't in the right place at the right time, but in the places where she was safe.

Even after he asked her to marry him, and she said yes, if it was O.K. with her folks, he couldn't get any further with her, and it got so he couldn't sleep right at night. Her folks said he had to have a job and have money saved. Pop and Henry kidded him about his Eyetalian girl, but they seemed to like her well enough. He told Doris you'd never catch him dead in the grocery business. There were the two jobs that weren't any good, and she was working too, and they both saved, and then he got the post-office appointment.

Even after the day was all set, she wouldn't let him. In fact, after the day was all set, she wouldn't let him do more than just kiss her. It was a great big wedding. Her folks spent a lot on it. There was a lot to drink, and a couple of the usual fist fights, and afterward they went on the train to Montreal. They had to sit up on the train, and they got to the hotel at eleven in the morning, and she said it was daylight and she wouldn't until night.

And when finally it happened, she acted like he was some kind of an animal or something. She acted like it was something she had to let him do because they were married. In the daytime when he'd just put his arm around her, she'd stiffen right up. It was the damnedest thing he'd ever heard of

She wasn't too bad while he'd worked at the P.O., but she'd certainly been mean and nasty since they'd been back at the store and since she got pregnant. And she'd got worse after Bonny had arrived. He'd watch Bonny and Doris would watch him watching Bonny, and there'd be a bad time after they got to bed.

Maybe Henry was dead, but he'd had a good deal there while he was on that leave and didn't come home. Hell, you could tell from looking at her that she knew the score. The way she walked and the way she was built. Henry always got the breaks. Pop had treated Henry right. You could tell Henry was the favorite son.

Everything went wrong for you when you weren't watching. Now it was like God spitting in your eye to have the two of them right in the same house. Bonny and Jana. They'd fixed it so he had to walk around looking at them all the time, and him married to a damn stringy stuffed dummy. It wasn't fair. None of it was fair.

But they were going to find out, all of them. He got up in the darkened room and knelt quietly by the bureau and pulled open the bottom drawer, inch by inch. He felt in, under the clothes, and touched the wedding portrait. He and Doris, standing there. She had no damn reason for ever sliding it out of the slot in the heavy yellow paper folder. It made him feel safe just to touch it. To touch it and think of the crispness of the fifty-dollar bills slid down behind the glossy print. There were twelve of them now. And a man could go a long way on six hundred bucks.

It had taken him since March to get hold of that many. There was no point trying to hold out on Doris on the money Pop gave him every Saturday night when he paid off the others. Doris wanted all of that.

So he'd gone about it another way. Between them, he and Jana did the bookkeeping, the way the accountant told them to. The problem wasn't to fool Jana. That was easy. The problem was to fool the machine. He had thought about a lot of different angles. Finally he found one so simple it had to work. Pop liked to pay the wholesalers in cash when they brought a bill around. The cash would come out of the register and the receipted bill would go in. Later Walter posted the bills to a ledger. He kited the receipted bills and took the difference from the register. A penciled figure one could be readily changed to a seven. Some of the bills had been made up on a machine. Those could not be altered. Pop seemed to have lost a lot of his intense interest in the business. The decline in profits would make little difference to him.

He closed the drawer and went back to the bed. Twelve paper pieces of freedom, and by the time Doris had to go to the hospital, he might have a thousand dollars.

He undressed in the darkness and got into bed. The ash tray clattered down between bed and wall. He left it there. Each night he went to sleep making up the same dream. He would be pacing a hospital corridor. They would come out and tell him that Doris had died in childbirth. Grief would turn him into a crazy man. They'd have to give him a sedative and keep him at the hospital. After she was buried, and after a reasonable period of mourning, he'd make a play for Bonny. She'd be feeling sorry for him. She'd comfort him. He wouldn't want to marry her, of course. Not after hearing what Rowell said, and the way he said it.

Then he went into the variation of the dream. The second shock of losing daughter-in-law and grandson would kill the old man. That would leave him owning the store, living in the same house with Jana and Bonny.

Then there was always the third possibility. Doris would have the kid, but on the day she was due to come home, he'd take off with Bonny. They'd head for the Southwest. Things were alive down there.

He could see the two of them. They'd pull up in the parking lot of one of those fancy gambling houses and park the convertible. Bonny would be a sort of a hostess. He'd have her wear long evening dresses, tight-fitting, made of gold and silver. And he'd wear a tux, midnight blue, and walk around through the tables and sort of keep an eye on things. The sharpies would stay away from his place. They'd know he wasn't the kind of guy you could fool with. Every once in a while he'd send a fat money order to Doris and the kid.

Tonight the dreams weren't working. Tonight the dreams were sour. He turned on the light and found his place in the book. Mike had just got the big blonde into his apartment.

Walter Varaki slid into a more comfortable position and began to read hurriedly. He was Mike Hammer. The grocery business was far away.

Chapter Five

MR. GROVER WENTLE was a very overworked gentleman. The high school was overcrowded. The teaching staff was barely adequate. And his secretary told him that Miss Forrest was waiting in the outer office with a disciplinary problem. It was the fifth time that day.

"Who is it?" he asked his secretary.

"One of the senior girls. Christine Varaki. Disturbance in study hall."

He started to say wearily, "Send her in and . . ." He stopped and stared at his secretary. "Teena Varaki? There must be a mistake."

"From the girl's attitude I hardly think so."

"Get me her record first. She's due to graduate in a few weeks."

The secretary sighed and plodded out. Mr. Wentle sat and remembered what he knew of Teena. Bright, capable, friendly. A good worker. Active in extracurricular activities. A rather sturdy, merry-eyed blonde, well liked by classmates and teachers.

The record brought to him was, surprisingly, up to date. The monthly grades had been posted. March had been her last good month. The grades for April and May were close to failing. He put the record aside. "Send her in. Tell Miss Forrest to return to study hall. It will be a shambles down there."

Teena came in. He saw at once that the look of sturdiness was gone. She was much thinner. Her face looked shallow. She sat facing him, without invitation, and her stare was bright and hostile.

"This doesn't sound like you, Teena."

"Doesn't it?"

The tone of her voice angered him. He waited until his temper was under control. "Suppose you tell me what happened."

"I was reading a book. Forrest came along. It's none of her business what I do as long as I keep quiet. She took hold of my hair. So I stood up and slapped her."

"You mean she just came along and took hold of your hair?"

"I knew she was standing there. She told me to put the book away. I didn't answer her. It's none of her business what I'm reading so long as I keep quiet. She took my hair to make me look at her. So I slapped her and she brought me here. I'll do it again the same way if she tries it again."

"This isn't like you, Teena."

"You said that once."

"I looked at your record. You were doing splendidly. What happened to you in March?"

"My brother died."

"I'm sorry. I didn't know that. This is a big school. It's hard to keep track of—"

"Don't sweat."

"What did you say?"

"I said don't sweat yourself up about it. March was a long time ago. He got killed in Korea. That's got nothing to do with this."

"With how your attitude has changed?"

"My attitude is all right. I like it fine."

"Others might not be as fond of it as you are."

"My attitude is my business. You want to expel me or send me back to study hall? Either way suits me. It doesn't matter."

"You don't care if you don't graduate?"

"Not particularly. I'll be eighteen this summer. I'm done with school."

"If you get your grades up during exams, I'm almost certain I can get you a university scholarship."

"Do I go home or go back to study hall?"

He looked into the hostile blue eyes and felt a sense of defeat. Sometimes you thought you had them, and then suddenly they were lost. There seemed to be more and more of them these last few years. Full of a new sullen hostility. Full of disrespect. He felt the weariness of his years and his position. In the dream he had planned to be a full professor by now, a departmental head at a college with a wide green campus, Gothic stone, chimes at sunset.

That was the dream. The reality was this ugly brick school, the hostile eyes, the evil, the obscenities. The reality was this girl who sat insolently slumped, insolently staring.

"Teena, if something is bothering you, I wish you'd tell me."

"Something is bothering me."

"What?"

"How the story comes out. The one I was reading when Forrest yanked on my hair."

"You come from a decent family, Teena."

"You want somebody should play soft on violins about now?"

"Go back to your study hall."

She got up and looked at him for a moment without expression, then turned and left his office, swinging her thin hips in the plaid skirt.

She got to the study hall just as the bell rang for the end of the period. Miss Forrest gave her a look of un-adulterated hate. Teena looked back with the flat in-difference of someone who looks at a door, window, chair.

She went down the aisle and scooped her books off her assigned desk and turned back toward the door. Fitz came up behind her.

"Make out?" he asked.

"Weeping Wentle made with violins."

"You're not out?"

She turned and looked back up over her shoulder at him. "Should I be?"

They went out into the hall. There was five minutes before the last class of the day. She leaned against the wall of the corridor, books hugged in both arms. Fitz leaned one hand on the wall and looked down at her.

"I got some sticks," he said softly.

"How many?"

"Enough. Ginny's got some caps. A hell of a lot of them. Bucky is all set with the car. How about it?"

"They want us along?"

"So why not? They want to pop. They want company. Ginny got the sticks and the horse. She says they're both real george."

"So why not? Like you said."

He bent his arm so that he leaned his elbow against the wall and thus stood closer to her. There, in the crowded corridor, between classes, he slid his free hand up under the hugged schoolbooks. She shut her eyes and made a small sound.

"Around the corner on Duval," he said, his lips close to her ear, "right after next bell."

He took his hand away and left her. She stood for a moment, the strength returning to her knees, and then walked down to her next class, getting there just as the warning buzzer sounded. She went to her desk, slammed her books down hard, and sat down, flatly returning the indignant stare of the teacher. The class whispered, giggled, rustled. The teacher stood up and the interminable last hour began.

Teena sat and thought about Fitz. She thought about Fitz and thought about what Ginny had, and wondered whether there'd be enough. It was funny how the two were getting all mixed up in her mind. Fitz, fix. Funny how she'd thought he was so messy before. Always doing fresh things. And always in trouble in schood. Running around with those girls they talked about. He and Bucky. Girls like Ginny. Ginny was nice.

The house had gone so sour when they heard about Henry. Like it had taken all the life out of the house, and out of her. All the life and all the resistance, so that when Fitz came around that same week, it didn't matter whether she went out with him or not. Bucky drove fast. Scary fast. And Fitz in the back with her. "No honey, You're not doing it right. Look. Like this. You put the cigarette in the corner of your mouth. See? But you got to leave your lips a little open so air comes in along with the smoke. Then you suck the smoke and air right down deep into your lungs. That's the kid! Come on. Again, now. That's the way, honey."

"I don't feel anything."

"Give it a chance, honey. Give it some time."

It was funny how fast it slowed the world down. She remembered how she could look at the speedometer and it said eighty, but looking ahead she could see every crack and pebble on the pavement, and it was as if she could hear the tick and thump of every cylinder in the motor. It was as if she could open the door and step out, the car was going so slow. Bucky had the place over the garage. His family had a lot of money. She remembered him saying that he was in public high schood because he'd been thrown out of the schools where they sent him. The place over the garage had always been a sort of play room for him. It was full of kid stuff. They'd ended up there, the four of them. Floating. The music was something that was new in the world. Notes like the slow ripple of silver cloth. All dim up there. Bucky's family away someplace. She smoked more, the way Fitz had taught her. And then Fitz had her watch Bucky and Ginny. Bucky heated a spoon over a stubby candle. She saw the gleam of a needle. Ginny stood with her face turned away. She worked her fist and Bucky held her arm tight and the blue vein came up, bulging ugly inside the delicate elbow. Ginny had funny black curly hair cut close to her head, and a cute shape and big wet brown eyes. She shook all over.

"What is he doing to her?" Teena had asked.

"Main-lining her. Capping her straight."

Time went all crazy. It would drag and then speed ahead. There was the music. Teena floated. There was just one dim bulb and the music. She and Bucky sat on the floor in front of the speaker. Fitz gave her another stick and she went far away then, and after a long time she awoke to an annoying, awkward discomfort. There was a heavy weight crushing her, and the weight was Fitz. The music was slow and hard in the ear. Fitz's eyes were so close to hers she could distinguish each separate lash. Bucky and Ginny were somewhere else in the room. . . .

When they let her out by her house, Fitz had to call her back to give her her schoolbooks. They seemed strange to her, a part of a faraway world that had lost all importance. She went into the alien house full of strangers, full of strange faces and alien eyes. The clock in her room said ten-fifteen.

The next morning she had remembered. Memory had terrified her. This house was the real world. These schoolbooks. That other was nightmare. The twelve blocks to school was the longest walk she had ever taken, and the sleet stung her cheeks, and she felt soiled and ashamed. She did not want to talk to Fitz. But she saw him in study hall, and made herself return his stare. Ginny had come up to her, later, in the girl's room.

"What are you looking so pink-eyed about, Teena?"

"I . . . I just didn't . . ."

"Watch the words around this outfit. We talked about you. You're a good kid, Teena."

"Thanks, but I . . ."

"The Christer types make me want to fwow up. You were a good sport. You didn't chicken on us."

"Maybe I should have."

"Relax. It's all for kicks. No damage done. We've got a party coming up. O.K.? See you at three."

And she found herself going with Ginny again, and again they drove fast, this time over ice, and ended up in the same dim room. From then on, house and school became unreal and stayed unreal. It was more comfortable that way. If you did not care, there was no place inside you that hurt any more.

She couldn't remember which time it was that Bucky gave them both the pops. Not in the vein, like he and Ginny took it. It wasn't like the sticks. This was something that rolled down hot through you and exploded, and ran right back up to a delicious floating warmth, a feeling of owning everything, a feeling of being queen of Hollywood, star of a show.

After a pop, the sticks seemed lifeless. Ginny and Bucky wouldn't come through again with a free cap for another pop when they were together again. They said they had a heavy habit to take care of. Fitz and Bucky quarreled. They made up, and there were a few more times when they were together again, and got a cap and a half apiece, having it cooked together, and Teena was crazy mad for a minute because Fitz got more than his half, but when it hit her, she got over being mad.

Now everybody had got mad again. The teacher droned on. She sat and thought about what Fitz had said. Sticks and horse. She thought sullenly, Horse for them and sticks for us. Meat for them and lollypops for us. But he had said they wanted company. Every time she thought of it, it made something turn over inside her. It had been too long a time. Three days. Her face was itchy and her eyes watered. It was funny about food. It would look good but you could chew and chew and it wouldn't go down. Ginny had left school last month.

The interminable hour finally ended. Another week gone. A week end stretching ahead.

The three of them were waiting in Bucky's car for her, where Fitz had said they'd be. She made herself walk slowly to the car. She could hardly keep from running.

She got in the back beside Fitz. "Hello, you people."

"The pride of Johnston High," Ginny said. "How you been making out, Teena?"

"Dandy. Just dandy.'

Bucky didn't start the car. He turned around and stared at Teena. Ginny stared too. It made her nervous. She tried to smile at them. She felt as if her smile were' flashing on and off like one of those airport things.

"I think it's O.K.," Bucky said.

"I know it's O.K. I told you it would be O.K.," Fitz said.

"What are you tlaking about? What's O.K.?"

They didn't answer. Fitz patted her leg. Bucky started the car up. "Where are we going?" Teena asked in a small voice.

"The family came back," Bucky said. "We're going to Ginny's place."

"Is your family away, Ginny?" Teena asked.

They all laughed at her, and it made her mad, so she sat back in sullen silence. Bucky drove downtown, past the railroad station, along a street of missions and cheap bars and shoddy hotels. He went down an alley and parked in a small concrete cavern behind an aged brick building. They went up back stairs for three flights. The air had a tired musty smell. Ginny unlocked the door of a small room with one window and they all crowded in. There was barely room for a sagging bed, bureau, and chair.

"Be it ever so humble," Ginny said. "Sit on the chair, Teena."

"Sure. Do we take a fix here?"

"Could be," Bucky said, giving her a cool crooked smile. Bucky and Fitz sat on the bed, side by side. Ginny leaned against the window frame and folded her arms.

"Why are you all looking at me like that?" Teena asked nervously.

"Well, it's like this. . . ."

"Shut up, Fitz," Ginny said. "I'll handle this. You need a fix, Teena?"

"Oh, God, Ginny! It's like things crawling all over me."

"How many free rides you got off us?"

"Gosh, I don't—"

"Plenty, kid. You think maybe it grows on trees? You

think you get it free because of your charming personality? It's time you started earning your fixes, dear. Like a good little girl."

Teena glanced from one to the other. They were all looking at her with a cold expectancy. "What's this all about?"

Ginny said, "I've made a few contacts since I quit that stinking school. I got a good source now. I can take care of you every time you want it. You can start taking care of your end of the deal right now."

"How?"

"There's a room right down the hall. There's a guy in the room. A friend of a friend. I described you. He paid for you, honey. He paid me. All you got to do is go down there and be nice to him. When you get back, the fix will be waiting."

Teena felt something shrinking inside her. "Somebody ... I don't know."

"Are you thinking you're better than me?"

"No, Ginny. No, but ..."

"What difference does it make? He's a nice guy. Room Thirty-eight, Teena."

"I ... can't."

Ginny crossed close in front of her, so close that her leg brushed Teena's. Ginny opened the top bureau drawer. She flipped open the little box and held it out. "All yours when you get back, honey."

Teena hugged herself. She felt cold. "I ... I can't."

"It's just the first time that's tough, Teena," Ginny said gently. "I got contacts. It's safe here. You ought to be able to take care of your habit with no more than four or five ... dates a week."

"Remember I get a fix out of this too," Fitz said worriedly.

Tenna looked at him. He was looking intently at Ginny, his mouth tight. "Because you roped her?" Ginny said. "You won't free-ride forever. And you got a bigger habit."

"So far," Bucky said softly.

"Shut up," Ginny said. "I'm running this." She looked at her watch. "You better get down there, kid."

"Give me the fix first. Then I'll do it."

"He specified no zombie, kid. You get it later."

They all kept looking at her. She got up slowly. She

felt as though she would break if she moved too quickly. She made herself think of how it would be, afterward. She made herself think of flame, spoon, and needle, and the wonderful tenseness of the last few seconds of waiting. She half heard Fitz's sigh of relief. She went out into the hall. "That way," Ginny said, pointing. "Thirty-eight."

She moved down the hall, feeling as if she were moving in a dream. The doorknob of Room 38 felt chill in her hand. She turned the knob and pushed the door slowly open. It was a room like Ginny's. A heavy man sat on the bed. He had a bald head. He had small dark eyes. He held a cigarette mashed between thumb and middle finger. He looked sharply at her, grinned, snapped his cigarette against the wall, and, standing up, said, "Come on in and close the door, honey."

Teena turned and ran, instinctively yanking the door shut in his face as she turned. She fled down the hall. She heard a harsh yell as she got to the head of the stairs. She went down the first flight so fast that she came up against the wall at the landing, stinging her hands. She was crying with fright so that she could barely see. She heard Ginny call her angrily, shrilly. She pushed open the heavy fire door that opened into the bright June afternoon. She ran down the alley and turned toward the railroad station. She sobbed aloud as she ran, and after she became aware of people stopping to stare at her, she slowed to a fast walk, and kept her face turned away from those she met. She looked back and thought she could see Fitz standing way back on the sidewalk.

When she reached home she went softly up the stairs to her second-floor room and shut the door. She lay on her bed. Every time she shut her eyes she could see him, see his grossness, see the bald head with the gleam of sweat.

And then her mind slid uneasily back to the look of the box Ginny had held out. And the crawling wanting began again, worse than before. She rolled her head from side to side. She held her fists hard against her forehead.

There was the box and the slick, sweet needle gleam, and the teaspoon, caked and blackened with delight, and the waxy stub of candle. She could have pretended the other thing was happening to someone else. Such a little unimportant thing to do to acquire something that would deliciously end the crawling want, the itching, the grainy eyes.

She heard Jana's warm mellow voice. "Telephone, Teena! You up there, Teena? Teena!"

Teena held her forearm across her mouth and bit it, making a pain she could barely stand. Jana stopped calling. Teena looked at the deep white notches in her arm that began slowly to turn red. She doubled her fist and hit her thigh as hard as she could. The pain knotted her muscles, cramped her leg. She wondered if they would give Fitz a fix anyway. Probably not. He'd be half wild by now. Suddenly she remembered the single stick she had hidden in her jewelry box. She had not wanted it before, wanting only the sick sweet swoop of the way the needle would hit, the way Bucky had fixed her in the vein the last time, drawing blood back up the needle and hitting her hard again.

Her hands shook and she had a terrible moment when she thought it was gone. Then her fingers touched the dryness. As she lifted it out, some of the contents spilled. She made a little paper scoop and took a deep breath and made her hands stop shaking long enough to pick up every shred and work them all back into the coarse paper tube. She lay on the bed and took the match and lit it and held it a moment and then touched the paper. She breathed as fast and hard and deep as she could, never taking the cigarette from her lips. The red line of burning climbed steadily up toward her lips. She kept it up until she had to pinch one tiny corner of the very end, until the last deep drag stung her lips.

She had been afraid of the distinctive smell of it in the house. But this was an emergency. She got up and disposed of the tiny butt that was burning her fingertips. She opened the windows wider, went back to the bed. It was, she thought, like being given spun-sugar candy when you wanted a steak. Like being hit with a handful of feathers when you wanted a sledge hammer swung hard against your heart.

The twisting need for the delayed fix roiled slowly under the surface easement of the stick, but it was a bit farther away. It was just far enough away to keep her from getting up and going back to the man in the room. It was just far enough away so that she was able, after a time, to trip and fall headlong into an exhausted sleep.

Chapter Six

RICK STUSSEN, the big fat blond butcher, thought of himself as an amiable man who, through no fault of his own, had got into a mess that seemed destined to get steadily worse until, finally, the whole world was going to blow up in his face. He spent a lot of time thinking about it. He would sit in his small back room on the ground floor of the Varaki house and he would tell himself that he would think his way out of this jam. And each time his thoughts would veer off into the past, and he would wonder how on earth this could possibly have happened to him. And sometimes he would cry. At such times the sheaf of bills hidden behind the loose section of baseboard was no comfort.

He was forty and he didn't know where the years had gone. He had come into the store when he was sixteen, when Walter had been a little kid, toddling around and getting into things. At sixteen, as now, he had been big around and blond, with rather small pink hands. He'd lived up on the third floor then, because the store took up most of the downstairs. Those had been the good years. From sixteen until the war came.

It had made him a part of something. And before that he had been a part of nothing. A part of gray yards where it always seemed to rain, and you were always lining up for something, and the sisters rustled when they walked. You cried when you were hurt, so the others were always finding new ways to hurt you.

Coming to be a part of the Varaki family was different. It was being a part of something. You could get out when you were sixteen if you had a job.

The bad years came right after he went to work, a year or two later. That was when Gus almost lost the store, and there was just Gus and Mom and him to handle everything.

It was good to be a part of everything and work hard and watch the kids growing up, Walter and Henry. Teena didn't come along until later. He always got along fine with the kids. Helping out. Staying with them when they were small and Gus and Mom wanted to go out.

He hadn't wanted it all to change. And that was the funny thing. People were always pushing on you, trying to push you out of the one place you'd found where everything was warm and soft and safe, and there wasn't any hurting.

The only hard thing had been getting used to the people in the store, coming in to buy. Gus had kept after him until he learned how you had to do it. Keep smiling and talk loud, and say something about the weather and try to remember their names. It wasn't too hard after you got onto it. It made you feel like you were hiding. You were hiding behind a big smile and a loud voice. He remembered the first few times he had been alone in the bathroom and happened to look in the mirror and see that big smile there, without even thinking about it.

It was Mom who kept pushing at him. "You got to get a girl, Rick. You got to go out. You got to get a girl and get a family."

"Sometime," he would say, smiling. "Sure. Sometime."

She had kept it up until he thought maybe it was the thing to do. She was a neighborhood girl. She was the only one he sort of liked the looks of, because she had a thin clean look. He remembered how hot his face got when he asked her for a date. They went out about six times. He didn't touch her. She seemed to like him. They laughed and smiled and joked around. And the Varakis kidded him about her. It was the sixth time they went out. The last time. He took her up on the porch and he was going to talk about the movie. She reached up and caught his shoulders and pasted her mouth hard on his, shoving herself against him. He flung himself wildly away from her so that they both nearly fell. She stood and didn't say anything. The hall light shone from behind her. She looked at him and then she went inside. She and her whole family stopped trading at the store. He couldn't tell Gus and Mom what had happened. It kind of scared him and made him half sick at the same time. Like the way he had scared himself a long time ago, back in that place. One of the sisters slapped him hard and he had to wear those bright red gloves for punishment for two days, even at meals. The mouth of the girl was somehow mixed up with the shame and the red gloves. So after a while they stopped talking about any girls.

He was drafted when he was thirty and sent to Fort Devon, where he spent two and a half years cutting meat in demonstration classes. It wasn't as bad as that place, but almost as bad. He made sergeant and got a room to himself, which helped some. He kept and used the smile and the laugh and the big voice. It would have helped if he had known that long ago. He didn't make any friends. He wrote Gus and Mom and the kids once a week. Teena was about seven then, Henry was twelve, Walter about sixteen.

Somehow it was all different when he got back. It had never been the same again. Somehow, in the two and a half years, he'd lost some important thing that had been there before the war. Something was barely out of his reach. The work was the same. He was a good butcher, and he knew it. Better, even, than Gus. The house was the same. They were all just farther away from him. He would sit with them in the small upstairs living room and feel closed out as he sat and smiled and nodded at things they said. It made him feel funny and he'd go up to bed, or go out and just walk. He wondered if the Army had made him restless or something. Like in that lecture they gave you when they discharged you.

He walked a lot and he was alone a lot. He had never been able to get any pleasure out of reading. So when he wasn't walking, working, sleeping, or eating, he would sit in his room.

There was a lot of work when the new store was built. It was as though building the new store had made things start to happen. Start to happen too fast. Mom got sick and died. Then that Vern Lockter came and took the delivery job. Walter quit his post-office job and came back with Doris, who never smiled back when he smiled at her. And he could hear them fighting a lot. Henry went in the Army. Anna, who never talked, came to cook and clean. Gus married Jana. Henry's wife came to stay. Henry got killed. Things were happening too fast and he wanted to hold out his hands and stop them.

But the bad trouble, the nightmare trouble, started after Vern Lockter came to work. At first it seemed fine. It seemed as though he was really going to have a friend, someone to talk to, the way Vern kept coming to his room and talking to him. He didn't seem like the kind of young fellow they'd put in jail. Vern would come and sit around in his room and make a lot of jokes. Rick couldn't understand all of them, but he always laughed anyway. And Vern used a lot of words Rick had never heard before. It was funny the way, at first, he had felt as though Vern was just a young fellow, and the way it sort of changed so that, unless he stopped and thought, it was like Vern was older. He told Vern a lot about himself. He told him about how it was in that place, long ago. And how it was before the war. And about his job in the war and all. He talked about how they used to hurt him back in that place. He started telling Vern how it was with the girl, but Vern started looking at him so sort of funny that he tried to make a joke out of it.

He couldn't remember exactly how he started going around to places with Vern. Vern had a lot of friends, all right. Vern taught him a lot of things. How to bowl and all. Then there was that place they started going, playing the five and ten poker game. Once he caught on to the game, he liked it. He liked spreading the cards real slow so that they came into view one by one.

It was all a lot better than before Vern came. He still couldn't see why Vern hadn't warned him that night about the game. It was in a new place. Vern had said he felt lucky and they went to the new place for poker. It was fixed up nice, with green on the table and chips that felt good. There were four men playing. They didn't say much. They looked important. Vern said it was a private club.

One of the men said, "Twenty-five and fifty all right for you gentlemen?"

Vern took Rick Stussen's arm and led him aside. "Think you can stand that?"

"Sure. Sure, I can stand it, Vern."

"Be lucky, then, big boy."

It was a real quiet game. The man who had spoken was banker. He handed Rick and Vern each a stack of chips. Rick reached for his money, but the man said, "We'll settle later, Mr. Stussen."

"Sure," Rick said, smiling. "Sure thing."

Rick was worried about the stakes, but when he took the first pot with a king-high flush, he began to feel more expansive. He won another pot, and then there was a long spell of poor hands and his chips melted away. When he was way down, the banker handed him two more stacks, one of reds and one of blues, and marked the paper again.

He saw that Vern would lose and then win. All the men played intently. Rick's second batch of chips melted slowly away, with the temporary respite of only one small pot. The man gave him a third batch, and Rick said, with nervous apology, "My luck keeps up like this, I better make this the last batch." He figured that at twenty dollars for each batch of chips, a sixty-dollar evening was pretty expensive.

"Maybe you ought to quit now," Vern said, looking worried.

"Maybe Mr. Stussen's luck will change," said the banker. He was a small man with a red face and fluffy white hair. There were purple veins in his cheeks and on his nose.

"I'll try one more batch," Rick said.

And the last batch began, dismally, to melt away, eaten up by the antes, lost in the purchase of cards that didn't help a pair.

When there were only a few chips left in front of him, the man on Rick's left dealt. He dealt very swiftly. Rick picked up his cards and spread them slowly. Ace, three, Ace, Ace. His throat felt tight. He slowly spread the last card until he could see the denomination. Ace. Give me some play on the hand, he said to himself. Give me some play on the hand.

The man on the dealer's left opened. Vern, the next player, stayed. The next man folded. The banker stayed. Rick said, "Just for luck I got to nudge that a little." He tossed out two blue chips.

The opener said softly, "I'm proud too. Back at you."

"I thought I opened this pot," the next man said. "Let's freeze out the ribbon clerks." He raised.

Vern tossed his hand in and said, disgustedly, "That makes me a ribbon clerk." The next two men stayed.

Rick said, "I better have another batch, please."

The man handed the chips over, marked the paper.

Rick said, "I'll try it again."

The dealer didn't raise again. He groaned and stayed. The opener raised again.

The man to the left of Vern who had folded earlier said, "Too rich for my blood, gentlemen."

The banker stayed and Rick, gloating inwardly, raised again. It was the last raise permitted him. The opener had one more raise coming. He used it. The banker stayed in and Rick stayed in. There were four of them left in. The dealer, the opener, the banker, and Rick.

"Cards, gentlemen?" the dealer said.

"I'll play these," said the opener.

"Pat hands make me nervous," said the banker. "I'll take one, please."

"One for me too," said Rick, discarding the trey.

"Opener bets," said the dealer, giving himself one card.

After the draw, the limit was two blue chips, three raises per player. Rick thought the dollars were landing out there in the middle with a pleasant abundance. The dealer folded immediately. Rick and the banker and the opener were left. The banker raised, Rick raised, the opener raised, the banker raised. It was two dollars to call. Rick put in three. Each man took his full quota of raises. As the opener was the last raiser, and both the banker and Rick called, he spread his hand and said, "Four delightful little tens, gentlemen."

The banker spread his hand. A flush.

"Four bullets," Rick said joyously, slapping them down. He reached for the pot. The banker encircled his wrist with small cold strong fingers. "A little fast, Mr. Stussen."

"What's the matter? Four aces beats tens, beats a flush."

"This kind of a flush, Mr. Stussen. Look again."

Rick looked again. He had missed it because they weren't in order. A three, four, five, six, seven of spades. Straight flush.

"A rough one to lose, Mr. Stussen," the banker said. He raked in the chips. They clattered into the wooden bin in front of him. "Very rough."

"I'm done," Rick said dully.

"I think I'm done too," said the man who had dealt. "We can't top that hand. Let's all settle up."

"What have you got left there, Mr. Stussen?" The banker asked.

Rick looked down. He felt dazed. "Three blues. One red. One-seventy-five."

"And you, Mr. Lockter?"

"My original stack and five blues."

"Two-fifty, then."

"That was a terrible beating," Vern said to Rick.

Rick forced a smile. "Four stacks I lost. All but one-seventy-five."

"Here you are, Mr. Lockter," the banker said. He snapped the bills as he counted them out. "One, two, three, four, five. Two hundred and fifty dollars. Correct?"

"Yes, sir."

Rick smiled broadly. By God, that was a good gag. Nobody seemed to notice his smile. Everybody seemed intent on the mathematics. Two of the other three players paid the banker. The man who had just dealt was paid off in hundreds and in fifties, to the amount of twelve hundred and fifty dollars, while Rick sat, still smiling automatically.

"I seem to be the big winner," the small white-haired banker said. "Mr. Stussen?"

"What?"

"Your liability seems to be exactly seven thousand, eight hundred and twenty-five dollars."

"I don't . . . I can't . . ."

They were all looking at him. He swallowed hard and smiled and said, "It was . . . like a mistake, I guess. I thought it was twenty-five cents. Fifty cents." He swallowed again and laughed. Nobody else laughed. "I haven't got that kind of money."

"I told you the stakes, for God's sake!" Vern said.

"Cents, you said, Vern. Cents!"

"I said dollars. Hell, I thought you could stand that. You told me you've been saving dough ever since you were sixteen."

"In the savings account I've got eleven hundred, almost."

The banker looked different. He didn't look as nice and friendly. His eyes were different. "People just don't do that to me, Stussen. They never have and they never will."

"Do what? Do what?"

"Come in here and try to make a killing without the money to back your losses. Nobody gets away with that

I think, Lockter, you better take your absurd friend over in a corner and tell him the facts of life."

Rick went over into a corner with Vern. Vern said, "My God, you played stupid! I thought you knew. Hell, I'll toss in my two-fifty, but that isn't going to help much. What have you got on you?"

"Fifty-two dollars, Vern. Honest."

"Don't you know who that guy is?"

"I forget his name."

"Karshner. They call him the Judge. He's never been any judge. He works for a very big guy in this town. The biggest. Karshner snaps his fingers and some boys come take you out and bury you in quick lime, Rick. Get your hands off me and stop blubbering."

"What am I going to do?"

"I don't know. Maybe you'll get a break. Maybe they'll just put you in the hospital for a long stay."

"Why? It was a mistake. I didn't know. Why?"

"Just as a lesson to somebody else who might try the same thing. I told you this was a rough game. If you'd won, you'd have taken the money, wouldn't you?"

"No. Just what I was playing for."

"You expect me to believe that?"

"It's the truth. Honest to God."

"You stay here. I'll go try to talk to him. It isn't going to do any good, but I'll try."

"Vern. You got to get me out of this. You got to."

"Stop sniveling."

He stood in the dark corner near a billiard table and watched Vern walk back toward the cone of bright white light over the green table and sit down. He couldn't hear what was said. Suddenly the four men got up and walked out of the room, leaving Vern sitting there. Rick heard their voices, heard one of them laugh as they went down the stairs. Rick went cautiously back to the table.

"What . . . what did they say?"

"Oh, shut up!"

"Vern, you got to tell me."

"Sure. I'll tell you. I brought you here. So whatever you get, I get too, you dumb son. They think I was in on it."

"But I'll tell them it was just me."

"Do you think they'd believe anything we say? Not a chance."

"What are they going to do?"

"I'll tell you what they said. They said we should sit tight. They know where to find us. They've got an idea. It seems that there's some friend of theirs needs a little help. If he can use us, then we can work it off that way. If not .." Vern shrugged.

"If not, what?"

"They send some experts around, Rick. Guys who know how to three-quarter kill you, and make the job last a long time."

"I'll do anything, Vern. Anything."

That was a long time ago. Nearly two years ago. He knew he'd never forget the fear of those two days of not knowing. When Vern at last came and told him he'd been contacted, and it was decided they could be used, Rick almost cried with gratitude.

The job was simple. After the first delivery on Monday each week Vern would return to the store with a package he got someplace. He wouldn't say where or how he got it. It was generally a small box, hardly bigger than a pack of cigarettes. In it was a bunch of little packets in the form of cylinders wrapped tightly in cellophane, fastened with layers of Scotch tape. He had to hide the little box somewhere around his working area. That wasn't hard. There were lots of places. Inside a carcass in the walk-in cooler. Behind the slicer. Lots of places. What was hard was memorizing the list. Nine names at first. Nine little packets in the box each week. Vern made him say the names over and over until he could say them in his sleep.

It worked like this: A phone order would come in. Walter or Jana or Doris or somebody would take it. There would be a meat item on the order. It was written out, name and all, by whoever took the order over the phone. When he made up the orders on his spindle, whenever he came to one of the nine names, he would have to slice a small pocket in the meat and shove one of the little cylinders in there. Then he'd wrap and tie and weigh the meat and scribble the price and the name on the brown paper. The nine people always phoned in cash orders.

For the first week he was too overcome with relief to question what he was doing. It was enough that he had to keep anybody from seeing what he was doing, and

keep remembering the names. But when the week end
came he found he had to know.

Vern wouldn't talk in the house, so they went for a
walk on Sunday, went to a park. It was a small park and
they found a bench away from other people.

"Now what's on your mind?"

"These little things in the meat, Vern. What are they
for? What are we doing?"

Vern gave him a look of incredulous contempt. "Just
how dumb are you, you big slob?"

"I'm sorry, Vern. I just wanted to know."

"You ever hear of dope? Snow? Junk? Big H? Horse?"

"Dope? Sure. There's dope fiends. They take dope and
commit crimes. I know about that."

"So what's in the little packages"

Rick stared at him. "Don't you go to jail for giving
it to people?"

"You go to jail if they find it in your possession,
Buster."

"Those nine people, then. They're dope fiends?"

"No. No. My God, there's enough in each package to
. . . Look. I suppose you ought to know what you're
doing. That's uncut stuff. Prime stuff. Those nine people
are pushers. They handle retail. We're in the middle,
between the wholesaler and the pushers. Now making a
meet is dangerous. That's what they call it when the
wholesaler contacts the pusher, gives him the stuff, and
gets the money. It's a cash-on-the-line business, all the
way up and down. We're working a gimmick. I figured
it out. I mean, somebody else figured it out, that the
most invisible guy in the world is a delivery man. I've
got a reason for traveling all over the city. I go in a place
with a big package of groceries. I've got money in my
pocket because I collect, too. I've got a record. Suppose
they shake me down. Are they going to dig around in a
piece of raw meat? The cover is perfect. I don't even take
the order when it comes over the phone. The pushers
pay me on the line, or I don't leave the stuff. What they
do then is their business. They cut it, cap it, and retail
it at about a hundred per cent profit—more, depending
on how much they can cut it and get away with it. They
use powdered sugar, other stuff. Rice flour. It's a sweet
delivery system, and they're willing to pay for it. I mean,
they're willing to forget that little trouble we had."

"Where does it come from?"

"We don't have to worry about that, do we?"

"But it's a bad thing to do, isn't it? I mean that stuff does bad things to people, doesn't it?"

Vern had clapped him on the shoulder. "You got to think about it this way: If we weren't doing it, somebody else would be. Isn't that right?"

"I . . . I guess so."

Vern handed him three ten-dollar bills. "What's this for?" Rick asked.

"Put it in your pocket. They think we're doing a good job. It's a little present. I got one too. There'll be a little every week."

After that there was fifty dollars every week. He had a sort of superstitious fear about either banking it or spending it, so he put it behind the loose section of baseboard, in against a joist. The names he had to memorize changed. New ones appeared on the list. The number of names changed. Once it was up to twenty. Twice, for no reason given Rick, there was no box, no packets. Those times Vern acted nervous. And when it started up again, it started slowly. Two, then three, then five packets a week. Growing slowly up to more than a dozen while Vern's good humor improved. Rick got so he could do it without thinking too much about it. He kept a few of the small shiny cylinders in his apron pocket. Some days there would be three names. Or one. Or none. He never played poker again. He did not go out at night with Vern any more. It made him nervous to be out at night. The shadows looked too black. Sometimes he dreamed about the man with the red face. Judge Karshner. The Judge sat on a high bench looking down at him, holding out a black cap, telling him to put it on and it would all be over.

The house and store had changed. Walter was sour and silent. The old man was gray-weary, lifeless, defeated —ever since the death of Henry. No one saw much of Teena any more. She was out late a lot. The new one, Bonny, was nice. Rick liked to look at her. He liked the way her hair looked, and he gave her his best smile. Henry married good, Rick thought. Not like that Doris.

The best part was when he was real busy. Fridays and Saturdays. Today was not good. Sunday. He sat in his room. The little radio made sad music, like water dripping. Gus had said a boy was coming to work tomorrow. A boy to help. That was good. There were things to do that Rick did not like. Cleaning up the trash, sweeping out, washing the big front windows, sorting out the bottle returns, fixing vegetable displays. The boy could go with Gus in the truck to the predawn farmers' market at the north edge of town, carrying to the truck the things Gus bought after his good-humored haggling. There were always so many little things. Taking care of meat scraps. Cleaning the hamburg machine. Marking cans with the grease pencil. Keeping the paper-sack racks full. Keeping the glass on the front of the meat case clean. He remembered when he had first come there, how gladly he had done all the little things, how glad he had been to feel the warmth of family around him. It was all changed, all different. Now he was not Rick the boy. He was Rick the butcher, living in the small downstairs room behind the kitchen. He was forty years old.

And I am a criminal, he thought. I can go to jail. It would be like that place long ago, and like the Army. Long lines and gray rain and stone.

He sat on his bed on a Sunday afternoon in June. His small pink hands were clasped between his knees. There was a tin-foil quality to the Debussy that the New York Philharmonic served him through the three-inch speaker of the green plastic table radio. He did not know he was wearing his habitual smile. He thought of the baby Doris would have soon. Maybe it would change the house. Maybe it would bring back the warmth. Maybe it would make things like the old days. The big house seemed very quiet. Anna was not in the kitchen.

He looked across at the photograph tacked to the wall. The old store, with all of them standing in front of it. The three kids, Mom, Gus, Rick. All smiling. It seemed like they had all died long ago. The music was a sound like gray rain.

Chapter Seven

VERN LOCKTER stood in the third-floor bathroom with a bath towel around his shoulders to protect his thin gray shirt. It was a blue-gray shirt made of Egyptian cotton, as fine as silk, tailored in England. It was new, and to wear with it he had selected the pale flannel slacks, so pale a gray they were almost white—the slacks with the small pleats and the side seams stitched in black. He wore a narrow green fabric belt with a small gold slip buckle, and green matching canvas shoes with heavy crepe soles and gold eyelets.

He turned on the water and waited until it ran warm, and then, making small cups of his hands, he ducked his head over the bowl and lifted the water to his hair, worked it in vigorously, making his scalp tingle. He turned off the water and opened the mirrored medicine cabinet and took out the narrow bottle of hair lotion. He poured a bit into his palm, rubbed his hands slickly together, and then worked that into the jet hair. With his comb he combed all the hair straight forward first so that it hung shining before his eyes. And then he worked it back, bobbing his head with each stroke starting from the top and working down to the hair worn long over the ears, using the more delicate strokes for that. He wiped the comb on a corner of the towel, replaced it in the cabinet, hung the towel on his rack. He took a small tube from the medicine cabinet and, using the smallest bit of vaseline on his fingertips, smoothed his eyebrows back. They had a thick gloss and almost met over the bridge of his nose. He took a cleansing tissue and wiped his fingertips dry. He examined his nails. They satisfied him. He inspected himself in the mirror. The fabric of the shirt was so thin that the weight of the fresh pack of cigarettes made the pocket sag. He transferred the cigarettes to the right pocket of the slacks, making a mental note to keep them there while wearing this particular shirt.

His body, under the clothing, felt sleek and hard and competent. Nothing, he thought, like running up- and downstairs with a few hundred pounds of groceries every day. He bunched his fist and flexed it and looked at the slide and change of the long muscles of the forearm. The black hair was curled thick on the top of his arm, running down the wrist to a thinner growth on the backs of his hands. There were small black tufts between the knuckles of his fingers. Once upon a time that had bothered him, offended him a bit. Then there was that college girl who had called it a "most intriguing and indicative secondary sex characteristic." He had made her repeat it and explain it, and he had filed the phrase away in his vast storehouse of memory. Later, following it up, he had brought the four books back from the public library. Freud, Jung, Adler, Stocklon. He had gone through them in a week. He had found them remarkably usable. And he found they repeated many things he had already half learned about people, and how to achieve from them the desired reaction.

His focus for twenty minutes had been upon himself. He stood and let his senses flow out. Bonny was closest, in her room down the hall. Since her coming the third-floor bathroom had held a faint effluvium of female. Cosmetics, racked toothbrush, a different brand of paste than he used. And, rarely, a long glossy dark red hair. He had picked one up, pulled it slowly between his thumb and fingernail, and seen it leap into a tiny coiled copper spring. Having her close had given him a constant awareness of her. She had filtered into his dreams. He had stalked her mentally, the way a man will play the market on paper, and estimated his chance of success. He could get no clear estimate. The factors involved seemed too variable. He suspected that it was because she was out of context. Misplaced. That blurred his vision. She was quite obviously knowing, aware, practiced, and disenchanted. Yet there seemed something hazy about her state of mind.

And so, with reluctance, he had restrained himself from making any trial advance. He sensed in her not only struggle and loneliness, but also that most dangerous thing, a disregard of consequence.

It would be stupid to imperil profit for the sake of impulse. And stupidity was the only crime. He had paid for that particular crime once. He did not intend to pay again.

It had taken him a month of steady dedicated thought to discover something about this business that could be marketed. It had taken him a week to make the contact once the idea was clear. He presented it to Karshner as a service he was willing to sell. Karshner told him he was too hot for such games. Wait until he was clear of Paul Darmond, the Preacher. And Karshner said it was a bad base, being in Rowell's back yard. But Karshner reluctantly took the proposition higher and came back with provisional approval, provided the butcher could be firmly hooked. Vern explained the plan for hooking him. Karshner said it was too complicated. Karshner suggested turning him into a user. Vern said he wouldn't work with a user any more than he'd try junk himself. It just wasn't safe. Karshner said he'd only suggested that to test Lockter's intelligence. Lockter told him that a recorded intelligence quotient of 140 was a pretty good test in itself. Karshner said he was a one-time loser and how bright was that? Vern said it was due to an impulse and he'd given up impulses.

Karshner said he would approve if he liked the hook. Stussen had been almost too easy. The next portion of the agreement was payment for the services to be rendered. That took time. The final agreement, satisfactory to all parties, was a fee of thirty dollars per delivery, with a guaranteed minimum of three hundred a week. The money was not, of course, to be banked or spent freely. That attracted attention. There was to be a weekly payoff to the butcher to make the hook more firm in the jowl.

The most delicate part of it had been the arrangement of the Monday-morning transfer, when Vern turned over the last week's cash, less his cut, for next week's box. That was the hottest point, the trouble point. That was where a tail could be operating from either end, ready to close in. There had to be a safe place for transportation of the box back to the store, and a safe place for the cash collections, which in a good week could total ten thousand. The same hiding place could serve for both, and it seemed logical that it should be on the truck. Yet it must be a place that would not be discovered were anyone else to drive the truck, or even work on it at a garage.

They did not like Vern's ideas, and he did not like theirs. In the end a false back was installed in the glove compartment of the panel delivery truck. It made the compartment shallower, but not noticeably so to anyone reaching in. It was pivoted off center and a firm push on the right end opened it. The transfer was made at a gas station where Vern had been refueling the truck prior to the arrangement. The men's room was small and rancid, and the door was around at the side. The key, on a piece of wood nearly a foot long, hung by the station door. On the wall of the men's room, placed high, was a rack for paper towels. It was battered, rusty, ancient. There was a newer rack below it, and that one was in use, taking a smaller-sized towel. It was highly unlikely that the old rack would be taken down. The upper edge was raised, so that on top of the rack was a depressed rectangle that could not be seen from the floor.

Each Monday Vern would remove the collection from the glove compartment while en route, a thick packet of bills from which he had already taken his end. He would shove it in his pocket, park the truck by the pumps, take the key, and go around to the men's room. He would lock the door behind him, reach high and take the box and replace it with the bills. He would put the box in his pocket, flush the john, run water, and, as an added touch of artistry, come out fixing his belt. As soon as he was en route again he would put the box in the secret compartment. Back at the store after deliveries were over, he would find a chance to slip the box to Rick Stussen.

During the moments of transfer he would feel as though all his nerves were being pulled fine through his skin, and as though he could never again take a breath that was deep enough.

He had simplified the marketing setup when he spoke to Stussen about it, leaving out one link in the chain. They were operating close to the top, close to the main source, the only source in Johnston. The deliveries were to the peddlers, rather than to the pushers. The farther down the line you got toward the ultimate user, the more dangerous it was, and the more careless and dangerous the people were. It was the job of the peddlers to supply the pushers, and they each had their intricate methods of transfer to the pushers. The final exchange, from pusher to user, was a raw blundering business of objects passed from hand to hand in lobbies of cheap theaters, in schoolyards, in broken-down candy stores, at dingy wrestling matches, on city busses. It was dangerous because too many of the pushers were users, and had become pushers in order to guarantee their own supply. They were unpredictable. And having to deal with the pushers made the job of the peddlers unenviable. But such were the profits all the way up and down the line that it was a risk that seemed to the peddlers to be worth taking. Vern had contempt for them. The contempt was proven to be accurate during the two bad times when the Man came to town in force and co-ordinated with the locals, and turned the peddling organization upside down, making a sweep of most peddlers and a lot of pushers but, almost inevitably, coming to a dead end at the level of the peddlers. The peddlers were kept under constant surveillance by the organization. They knew that at the first sign of addiction they would be cut off at the pockets and a new peddler lined up. And they also knew that if they cracked and gave away source and method once they were taken in, they would sooner or later have a bad accident. In prison or out.

It was nice, and it had been nice, and it had gone smoothly, and there had been a few bonuses from time to time. There was a place in the cellar, in one end of the cellar, where the floor had not been concreted. There were three fruit jars buried there, the black dirt tamped hard over them. In them the money was rolled tight, and it was good to think about them. Stained moldy money could mean trouble. He had dripped the wax thick around each lid in addition to the rubber gasket and spring top. All used bills in smaller denominations. A fourth jar, hidden behind cellar trash that hadn't been touched in years, was slowly filling. By the time it was full there would be close to forty thousand.

He went back over the new problem. That was what caught so many of them. They would sense a factor that could disrupt the whole thing. Yet the thought of the money coming in blinded them. Just a little more. Just a little bit more. Then I'll quit. That was the blindness that spoiled everything. You had to be alert for the smallest cloud on the horizon. Then forget the money. Predicate the risk. Figure the odds. And if it looked bad, get out and get out fast.

It would be difficult to cut loose right now. The delivery system had made them too happy up there on topside. It had made them feel too safe. So any reason he could give would not be enough—particularly the reason that was in his mind. They would laugh at that one. The ideal situation would be to blow the whole arrangement sky high without imperiling himself. That couldn't be done by a double cross. Their arms were too long. They could reach too far. And leaving Stussen behind would mean an almost automatic warrant.

The ideal solution would be to have Stussen drop out. Drop all the way out. Drop dead. Then there would be no possibility of carrying on. The time lag of setting it up in the same way again would be too great. The market had to be supplied. So they'd have to go back to the previous, more risky method of supplying the peddlers. And that would be an automatic out for one Vern Lockter.

But Stussen wasn't going to oblige by dropping dead merely because it was convenient. And killing was a task performed by a fool. So, to eliminate one fool it was necessary to convince a second one that it was a job worth performing. That, in turn, brought the slow wheel back to Jana, where it stalled against the immutable fact of Stussen's sexlessness.

It was a convoluted problem, and it made him tingle with awareness to consider the aspects of it, to consider potential solutions. He had confidence he would find one.

But first it would be necessary to examine the new problem a bit more closely, to see if perhaps he was exaggerating its importance. He knew that he had been guilty of a minor bit of stupidity. For a time his awareness of every detail of his environment had been faulty.

It was Friday evening, two days ago, that he had gone up the stairs and stopped at the second-floor landing, stopped very still, his nostril widening as he detected, to his astonishment, the faint cloying odor of weed. He had stood there, and known in a matter of seconds. The kid. Teena. Much quieter lately. Out a lot. Thinner. Quite a change since the death of that Henry, Gus's

precious Henry, the oaf in uniform. On Friday he had
told himself it was all right. If the kid was on tea, the
word could be passed along, topside to peddler to pusher.
Cut her off at the pockets. They roped them with tea
and built them up to horse. Tea could be dropped without a cure. Horse couldn't. And throw just enough of
a scare into the kid to make it stick. If she got on horse
and turned wild, that unfunny man with the unfunny
face would lean hard. He might lean hard enough to
tip something over.

So, on Saturday, he made a point of getting a good long
look at Teena. And he found she was beyond tea, found
that she had a habit. Perhaps it was a small one com-
paratively, but she was starving for it. The signs were
there to read in the reddened eyes, the tight movements,
the yawning, the rubbing of the nose. She'd been out
Saturday night and he hadn't seen her yet today, but he
hoped she'd connected somehow. It would make her
easier to talk to.

He walked down the hall from the bathroom to the
stairway, and heard, in passing, the muted sound of the
music Bonny was forever playing softly on that record-
player of hers. He had heard Rowell had leaned on her.
That was fine. He could lean that way all he wanted.
Vern saved the same look for Rowell that he used on Paul
Darmond. Bright young man who has learned his lesson.
Direct look and shy smile. Darmond bought it. It couldn't
be sold to Rowell.

When he thought of Rowell, he thought of seeing the
clown face on the ground and stamping hard with his
heel, turning it as he stamped. The thought made his
shoulders come up and flattened his breathing. No. That
was in the impulse department. That was glandular. Not
out of the head. Discard everything that doesn't come
out of the head. Discard that thing that can come roaring
up through you like black flame. That's what happened
the last time, when you smashed the stein and jabbed
with the broken handle and felt the glass shards twist and
tear the soft tissue of the face that had sneered, had an-
noyed you.

The flame died quickly away, and he went catfooted
down the stairs, feeling the flex of his body, feeling taut,
aware, all his senses standing open like doors, intensely
aware of himself in space, in time, in precise moment of

time. Bonny upstairs. Walter, Doris, Gus, Jana, and Anna all off at the afternoon movie. Rick Stussen down in his tiny room off the kitchen.

He went softly down the hall to her door and pressed his ear to the varnished panel as he slowly turned the knob. He heard her bed sigh as she moved, heard a soft cough. He opened the door quietly and stepped inside and shut it quickly enough to contain her gasp of shock and surprise.

"Don't come in here!"

"I'm in. I want to talk to you."

She was in pajamas and robe, her hair rumpled, her face wan. She sat up, tugging the belt of the robe tight, unconsciously combing her hair back off her forehead with her fingers, giving her head a quick feminine toss.

"Get out! You can't come in my room. I'll yell."

"Wouldn't you rather yell for a fix, Teena?" he asked.

Her shoulders came slowly forward and she looked crumpled, sitting there. "A fix? I don't know what you mean."

He took two quick steps, snatched at her left wrist, shoved her sleeve up roughly. "A fix. A cap. A jolt. A pop. What do they call it in your group, dear?"

She looked down at the floor. He released her wrist. Her arm dropped limply. The sleeve slid part way down.

"How long has it been?" he asked, sitting beside her on the bed.

"Five days."

"Trying to break it cold?"

"God, no!" She still stared at the floor. He caught the faint stale flavor of her breath. "How did you find out?"

"Just like when I pick up a newspaper. I know what the news is because I can read the print."

"It doesn't show that much."

"Not to those who don't know what to look for. You had weed here in your room Friday. It stinks. I smelled it."

"It was the only thing I could get hold of."

"Couldn't you make a connection last night?"

"I couldn't find anybody. I'm sick. I'm awful sick, Vern. I had a connection Friday and walked out on it. I can't stop thinking about it."

"Walked out when you were three days hungry?"

"Stupid. I keep wishing I could set the calendar back to

Friday." She turned sharply toward him in sudden aware-ness, and her sharp fingernails bit his wrist. "You know the score, the way you talk. Vern, have you got any? Have you? Do you know where I can make a connection? Please, Vern. Please, I'm dying."

"Just shut up and answer questions. What was the last fix?"

She turned a bit, her back half toward him. "Cap and a half."

"Main-lined? Yes. I saw the new marks. Kid, do you want to kick the habit?"

"Right now, yes."

"How do you mean, right now?"

"I do and I don't. I can't explain. Sometimes I think of what's happening to me. I mean, the way it's making me look. Then I want to kick it. But not cold. A taper. Then . . . Oh, hell, Vern. What's left if I do? What's left for me? I've already spoiled one kind of life, and there's only the other kind. Nothing in the middle."

"What were you thinking about when I came in?"

"Killing myself. I was thinking about different ways."

"That would be a nice mess."

"It would be easier than the way I feel. I spoiled my only connection Friday. I don't know how to get another one."

"Maybe I can do something."

She turned quickly and he saw her immediate misinter-pretation, written shrill across her eyes. "I'll do anything you want me to do, Vern. Anything. Honest to God."

"I don't mean that. I'd like to see you kick it. You'll feel different when you're out from under. God, you're seven-teen and you look twenty-five."

"I know."

"I can't get in touch with the right people until to-morrow. Then I might not hear for a couple of days."

"I can't stand it that long. I can't stand it."

"I don't mean for a fix. I mean for a way to get you off it. If things work right, you can play sick and—"

"I won't have to play hard."

"Shut up and listen. Play sick and I can maybe get hold of the right doctor. One who won't tell your old man the score. Just tell him you're . . . well, on the verge of a nervous breakdown and ought to go into a rest home. You'll get a cure."

"No."

"I tell you, you'll get a cure. It's not hard. They taper you off. They use other drugs that cut down the shakes."

"They all say it's terrible."

"I want your solemn promise that you'll play ball with me on this."

"I can't stand it that long. I'll go crazy. I'll do something terrible."

"Suppose, in return for your promise, I get you enough to tide you over."

She grabbed his arm. "Can you? Right now? Can you?"

"What about your promise?"

"Oh, yes, Vern. I'll do it. I told you I'll do anything."

"A junkie's promise. You know what that's worth."

"Cross my heart, Vern."

"You won't leave the house until you leave with the doctor?"

"No, Vern. No. Get me a strong fix. A heavy one. I need it."

"You got an outfit here?"

"No. I was wishing I had. I was going to put a bubble in my blood. They say that kills you easy."

"Stop that kind of talk."

"All right, Vern. Anything you say."

"You understand I'm taking a hell of a risk. I'm doing it because your old man gave me a break. I don't want you to break his heart."

"Hurry, Vern. I promised. Go get it for me."

He went out into the hall and shut the door quietly. He recognized all the dimensions of the risk he was taking. Yet, all in all, it seemed to be a lesser risk than letting her go off, fly apart, or remake her own connection until her habit got so big it ruined her, turned her into morgue bait or a face in a line-up. In either case, Rowell would be snuffing around. This way—and certainly topside would see the necessity for co-operation—no one should be the wiser, and the kid would get a cure that she would think was the result of human kindness.

He knew he might not have much time. Yet he had to pick the safest peddler in the book. He went silently through the kitchen and let himself into the store. The red neon around the wall clock burned all week end, as a night light. He found the book under the counter and looked up the number.

Chapter Eight

AFTER THE FOURTH RING a woman answered at the number Vern Lockter called. "Is this Mrs. Fallmark?" Vern asked cautiously.

The answer was equally cautious. "Yes. Who is this, please?"

"Mrs. Fallmark, this is Varaki's Quality Market. We've just been checking our records and we find that on the order that was delivered to you yesterday, the canned cat food wasn't included. You paid for it as part of the order, but it was left out by mistake."

"But I'm positive it was—"

"This is Vern, the delivery boy, ma'am."

"Oh. Would you mind holding the phone a moment? Let me check and make sure. I can almost remember putting it away."

He stood in the silent store, holding the phone. She came back on the line. "I could have sworn I put it away."

"We didn't want you to be caught short, ma'am."

"Will you deliver it Monday, then?"

"It's no trouble to run out with it right now. I have to come out that way anyway. I'll be out in fifteen minutes."

"All right, then."

He hung up, pleased with the way he had handled it. There had been four cans of cat food on the Saturday order. If the phone were tapped, that would check with the order. He put four cans of cat food in a paper sack, went back through the house, and got in the truck.

Mrs. Fallmark lived with her juvenile husband in a residential district that had once been fashionable. The house was pseudo Moorish, finished outside in a weary shade of yellow cement plaster. He turned into the drive and parked behind a dusty new Buick. He carried the sack onto the back porch of the house and rapped on the

74

screen door. The inside door was open. A cat peered around the corner of the kitchen doorway, looking down the short hallway at him, legs crouched.

Mrs. Fallmark came to the kitchen doorway. "Bring it right in, Vern," she said. She was a heavy matronly woman with a blue-purple tint to her gray hair. Her hair was always so carefully waved that it looked carved from stone.

He walked in and set the sack on the kitchen table. The cat stalked around him.

"What's this all about?" she demanded. "What are you doing here on Sunday? I'll be damned if I like it."

"I'll be damned if I have any interest in your opinion. I want four caps and a hypo."

"I don't retail."

"Right now you do. And it isn't retail. It's a free gift."

"Who do you think you are, Vern?"

"I'm the delivery boy. This is an emergency. I got orders from topside. Pick it up from you. They don't want me contacting any pusher. They said come to you. And just incidentally, if it came to a case of their getting along without me or without you, who do you think they'd pick? Don't let the fact that I bring groceries go to your head. I either get the four caps and the hypo in three minutes, or you get cut off at the pockets."

"Big talk!"

He went over and leaned against the sink and lit a cigarette. He looked at his watch. The cat nuzzled his leg with the side of its head. "Suit yourself," he said.

"An emergency?"

"A user who might spoil the delivery setup."

She turned heavily and walked out of the kitchen. She was back in a few minutes. She handed him a new hypo in the original plastic and cardboard case in which it had come from the druggist. The seal was broken. He slid the box open and saw the caps and slid it shut.

"Thanks for being so obliging, Mrs. Fallmark."

"You go to hell."

He stood inside the screen door, looking out. The street was empty. He got in the truck and drove back to the store. He had been gone forty minutes. He saw that the ancient Varaki sedan was parked behind the store. The timing had gone bad. It made it a little tougher. As he came in the door Gus called him. "Vern? Vern, that you?"

He went to the living-room door. "Believe it or not, I had to make a delivery. You owe me overtime, Pop. That Mrs. Fallmark called up and said we forgot to put in the cat food on yesterday's order."

Walter was squatting in front of the television set. He looked back over his shoulder. "The hell she says! I made up that order. I put that cat food in. Four cans, or six. I forget."

Vern smiled and shrugged. "So she mislaid them. So we lose four cans of cat food. She's a good customer."

"Every week a big order," Gus said.

"A good program is coming up, Vern," Walter said.

"I'm taking me a nap. Hard night last night."

He went back into the kitchen and got a noisy glass of water. While the water was roaring into the sink, he used the cover of the sound to take a spoon from the silver drawer and slip it in his pocket. He went up to his third-floor room and stood in the silence for a moment until the rib-cage fluttering died down. He had heard Bonny's music still playing, as he came down the hall.

He shut his door as he left his room, and went as quickly and silently as he could down to the second floor. He could hear the gusts of mechanical laughter coming over the television downstairs. He hoped it would hold them down there.

He went into Teena's room and she came up off the bed, drawn as tight as harp strings. Her whisper was too aspirated. "You got it?"

He nodded. He went to her dressing table and opened the box. She stood close beside him, so close he could hear her hard fast breathing. He fitted the hypo together, held the sharp tip briefly in his lighter flame.

"Can you do it?" she whispered.

"I've watched it done."

"I've never given it to myself. God, we've got to be careful." She went to her closet and came back with a thin red belt, which she wound tightly around her left arm, above the elbow. He had poured the white powder, faintly yellow-tinged, into the bowl of the spoon. He set his flaming lighter on the corner of the dressing table. She said, her voice shaking, "You cook and I'll fill the hypo, and take it off the fire when I tell you, or it'll be gone. Then you take the hypo quick and do it."

The powder over the flame moved, changed, melted.

"Now!" she said. He took it off the flame. Her hands shook badly. "Hold it steady, Vern. Please." She filled it, handed it to him, worked her fist. The scarred vein bulged blue in the milky socket of the elbow. He held the needle up, pushed on the plunger until a drop stood yellowish on the point.

"Hurry," she said. "Oh, God, hurry!"

He felt awkward, faintly ill, as he slid the tip into the vein. It was harder to puncture than he had thought it would be. He bit his lip. he watched, her mouth working. She looked like thin gray lines drawn on pale paper. He pushed the plunger slowly and emptied the calibrated tube into her blood. He pulled the needle free and watched her.

She stood braced, her eyes half shut. Her pale upper lip wormed upward over her teeth in a look that was savage and sexual. For a moment the whites of her eyes showed, the pupils rolled upward. The red belt slid, like a slow snake, to the floor. Hungry nerves fed on the drug and were mended. Her color changed. She looked at him and her eyes were soft and her mouth was soft. "Aw, Vern. Aw, honey!" she said in a sleepy, lazy voice. "Aw, how I needed that!" She went to her bed, seeming more to drift than to walk.

He stood there, feeling a refinement of the sense of power, feeling a hard domination. It made him feel bigger and stronger than anything that had ever happened to him. With this you could control another human being utterly, completely. She sat flushed on the edge of the bed, rocking slowly from side to side in beat with music only she could hear, and she looked through and beyond the high corners of the room. It was, he thought, like having a woman, only more so—distilled, intensified.

It was like something that had happened to him a long time ago, back in that faraway town of slag heaps, of rows of smoke-dingy identical houses that were set on the dirt shoulder of the deep ravine, that town where the coal dust was pocked deep in the faces of the heavy-shouldered men.

Two gangs of boys had been fighting each day after school, down in the ravine, down among the tough weeds, the twenty-year accumulation of trash thrown from the back porches of the houses down the slope. They fought with rocks, with air rifles, with slingshots. Vern had been alone, not a part of either gang, spying on both sides, moving too fast and too quietly to receive hurt, aiming carefully, hurling, then melting away into the brush, content with the yowl of pain and outrage behind him.

He had found the piece of sharpened steel rod, quarter inch, rusty, nearly two feet long. He put the blunt end in the pouch of his slingshot. He could pull it back until the sharpened tip rested in the fork of the wood. He crept up on the battle lines that afternoon, tense with excitement. He wiggled around a mound of debris and saw, startlingly close, just below him, a boy lying face down, peering along the barrel of an air gun. Vern was ten. The boy was fourteen. He didn't know that then. It told about him in the paper the next day. The sharpened tip of the steel rod went through the upper tip of the boy's ear and into his head. The boy let go of his gun, rubbed his face against the ground, scrabbled with his hands. He humped up in the air like one of those green worms and was motionless for a moment, as Vern watched, then slowly flattened out against the stony ground. None of his movements had dislodged the steel rod. Vern snatched it free and moved back toward his home, toward the high dirt bank. He went up a gully, unseen by anyone, and part way up he shoved the steel rod into the dirt, pressed the last few inches out of sight with the heel of his sneaker. He went up the shed roof and into his room, brushed the dirt off his clothes, and came slowly down the stairs into the kitchen. His mother stared at him. "I thought you went out."

"No. I was looking at a book."

"If you're going out, stay out of the ravine. It's filthy down there and those boys'll hurt you. They're too big for you to play with."

He stayed on the high slope. He heard the yells and fifteen minutes later he heard the siren. Then he went down. The other gang had scattered. They had a hard time getting the boy out of the ravine. Finally one of the ambulance men took the boy over his shoulder. The boy's arm dangled loose. His hair was long on the nape of his neck. He had needed a haircut. Vern watched all of it. It all gave him the same feeling he had now, watching the girl sitting on the bed, swaying slowly in her private world.

He looked at the girl and thought how fine it would

be to continue this, to keep getting it for her, to keep
making it happen again and again. To watch closely each
time that spasmed change in her.

He took the needle apart and put it back in the box.
The lighter had gone out. He snapped it shut and put it
in his pocket. The routine actions brought him back to
calmness, and he rejected the impulse. He thought she
would object to his taking the outfit away. She did not
even seem to notice that he was leaving. He closed the
door behind him, after making certain the hall was clear.
He went down the back way, through the empty kitchen,
and down the cellar stairs. He hid the outfit beside the
unfilled jar behind the pile of ancient trash.

The good feeling he had as he watched her had left him
with a restlessness. The day was nearly gone as he went
out the back way onto the street. He touched his hip
pocket with his fingertips. There was fifty dollars in his
wallet, he remembered.

He caught a downtown bus at the corner. When the
bus crossed the invisible line of Rowell's precinct, he felt
better. This was one night when he did not want Rowell
leaning on him. Make one mistake and they never let you
alone. Tomorrow Darmond would be bringing the new
kid around. Once this current problem was settled, it
might be interesting to sound the kid out. He might turn
out to be a useful type. It might be possible to shove a
little of the risk off on him. Minimize risks. Maximize
profits. Calculate all risks. Avoid impulse.

He began mentally to compose the note he would leave
with the week's collection the next morning, on top of
the towel rack.

Chapter Nine

AT FIVE MINUTES of ten on Monday morning, Paul Darmond stood near the magazine stand and watched the people coming out of the gates from the train that had been announced as arriving a few minutes before.

He saw Jimmy Dover come into the station, put his battered blue canvas zipper bag on the floor, and light a cigarette with elaborate casualness, shake the match out, and then look slowly and warily around the station waiting room. He looked more gangling and awkward than he had in the reform-school denims, and Paul realized it was because the boy's chest and shoulders had thickened while he was at the school, and the gray jacket with its faded team emblem was too small for him.

Paul could guess how the trip down had been, how the boy must have tried to appear casual about staring out the train window. The boy saw him and picked up the bag and came toward him, unsmiling.

Paul advanced to meet him. This was the ticklish time, this first meeting outside the school. It would set the pace of their entire relationship. The fact that the boy had not smiled on seeing him was something to bear in mind.

He smiled and put his hand out. "Hello, Jimmy."

"Hello, Mr. Darmond." The boy took the offered hand somewhat shyly, released it quickly.

"Coffee?"

"Sure. I guess so."

They went into the station restaurant and sat on two stools at the counter. "Have a good trip?"

"It was all right."

"Would you rather have a Coke?"

"Coffee is fine."

They did it to every one of them. Forced them to build the wary walls, something to hide behind and peer over.

Something to duck quickly behind. Adolescence built its own wall, for both the free and the caged. This boy had a good face. Square lines. A firm chin. Level brows. Carsey, at the school, had recommended him for freedom before his time was up. Carsey's recommendations were generally good.

The waitress brought the coffee. There was a tenseness about the boy, an air of waiting for something unpleasant. Paul knew how the boy had classified him. A do-gooder. A giver of moral lectures. The man who could send him back at any real or fancied slip. Better than average intelligence, Carsey had said.

He decided to take a chance on the boy's intelligence. "This is the place, Jimmy, where I'm supposed to explain the difference between good and bad, and ask you if you've learned your lesson, or words to that effect."

The boy turned his head quickly and gave him a look of surprise. "What?"

"Tell me, do you feel like a lecture this morning?"

He saw the threat of a smile, immediately repressed. "I guess not, Mr. Darmond."

"Carsey no doubt gave you that business about not letting me down, and him down, and Gus Varaki down."

"He sure did."

"That's the standard line. We appeal to your sense of loyalty. Actually, Jimmy, it's a calculated risk. Think of some of the guys up there who'd be bad risks. Can you think of some?"

"God, yes!"

"We calculate our risk on the basis of a lot of factors. We considered your environment, which wasn't good. The death of your parents, which was unfortunate. We considered your adjustment to the school, your intelligence, your leadership abilities, your personality. On that basis we decided to take the risk. We're good at evaluation. We don't miss often. When we do, they give it a lot of publicity. You've been evaluated as a good risk. So I don't want to mess with your emotions. How you feel about all this is your own business. If it works, we'll be glad. If it doesn't work, you're a statistic. Get what I mean?"

"I . . . guess so."

"So no lectures today, Jimmy." He saw some of the defensive tension go out of the boy. "I'll answer any questions you might have."

"How often do I have to report to you, sir?"

"We won't make that a routine. If you have a problem, you can get in touch with me. I drop around at the store once in a while. You can't change jobs or where you live without informing me first."

"One thing I've been wondering. I don't get it. Why does Mr. Varaki give me a room and a job?"

"Forty years ago Gus Varaki was in bad trouble. Somebody gave him a break. He's been paying it back over the years. You remember my speaking about Vern Lockter last time I talked to you? Gus took Vern under his wing two years ago. Vern lives there too. He's on his own now, the way you'll be when one year is up. He's stayed out of trouble. He drives the delivery truck. Gus took his butcher, Rick Stussen, out of an orphanage twenty-four years ago. Gus lost one of his sons in March. He hasn't snapped out of it yet. So don't worry if he acts a little strange."

"That's tough."

"Korea. Next year you'll be registering for the draft, once you're out from under my wing."

"Maybe I could enlist then."

"Why, Jimmy?"

"Well, I've only got one year of high. That isn't much. It's pretty tough to handle a job and night school too. I want to look into that, though. I was reading about how they extended this G.I. Bill. That would give me a chance to catch up, I mean after I got out."

"What gave you this yen for education?"

Jimmy glowered at his coffee dregs. "I guess it was that bunch of punks up there."

"Can you control your temper, Jimmy?"

The boy looked at him. "What do you mean? Sure. I guess so. I don't get mad often."

"There's a police lieutenant named Rowell."

"I heard about him."

"The market is in his precinct. He'll leave you alone for a week or so. Then he'll come around and he'll give you a bad time. He'll try to make you sore. He'd like to make you sore enough to take a punch at him. Then he could send you back and laugh in my face. He doesn't think anybody ought to be let out until his time is up, and he doesn't like it even then. He says boys like you are incapable of ever being anything but criminals. He goes around trying to prove his point."

"He won't make me sore, Mr. Darmond."

"Then let's go get you settled, Jimmy."

On the way to the west side, Paul drove slowly and briefed Jimmy on the people who lived in the big shabby old house. As he went through the list in his mind, he had the feeling that he had left someone out, yet he knew he hadn't. It seemed there was something missing in the house, something that should be there if it were to be a proper place for Jimmy Dover to recover his confidence, his self-respect. There seemed to be a drabness, a sound of defeat in the list, and he realized that he had subconsciously thought of the Varaki house as still containing the dead mother, the dead son. All at once he had the strong feeling that this was perhaps a mistake—that Gus was making an offer of something he no longer possessed, the sense of warmth and household unity that he had wanted to share in years past.

But once they were there Gus's greeting made Paul Darmond forget his uncertainty. Gus talked loudly in his distorted English, laughed, patted Jimmy's shoulder as he introduced him around. Walter, Bonny, Rick, and Jana were in the store. Walter's greeting was the only one that seemed a bit cool.

Anna, in the kitchen, favored the boy with one grave, monolithic nod. Doris, in the living room, was waspishly polite. Vern was out on delivery. Gus labored first up the stairs, saying, "You go on third floor, Cheemee. Not big room, but clean. Good bed. Bonny and Vern, they are on third floor. Me and wife and Walter and Doris and Anna and my Teena, all on second floor. Rick in back room way down." Gus proudly showed the room, saying, "You like, Cheemee?"

"It's swell, Mr. Varaki."

"No mister. I am Pop. I am Gus. I am no mister. You unpacking, then no work today. Look around. Take a look at the neighbor houses. Tomorrow is work quick enough, you bet anybody." Gus stood for a moment and Paul saw his eyes go dull as he seemed to look into distant places. The life seemed to drain out of the man.

"This is fine, Gus," Paul said.

"Er? Oh, sure. Hope the boy likes. Plain food here. Plenty of food, you bet anybody." He jabbed Jimmy in the ribs. "I take you buying in the morning. Still dark. You learn something new, eh?"

"Sure."

"Come down now and meet my Teena. Home from school today. Not feeling good."

"Maybe we shouldn't bother her now, then," Paul said.

"Is not bother."

They followed him down the hall on the floor below and he banged noisily on Teena's door. "Teena! Come meet new boy friend, Cheemee."

They heard her faint answer and soon the door opened. She stood, unsmiling, in the doorway. It had been many weeks since Paul had seen Teena and the look of her shocked him. It took only a moment before the second, much greater shock hit him. He had seen a lot of it. The dull look of the oversized pupils of her eyes. The graininess of skin, the dullness of hair, the sleepwalking look. It seemed incredible that Gus could not see it. Yet he supposed she had changed slowly while Gus was lost within himself, lost in the endless mourning for his son. He knew at once that he had to do something, and do it quickly.

"Teena, this is Cheemee Dover."

"Hello" she said tonelessly.

"Hi," Jimmy said, unsmiling.

"You need new boy to go to movies with, eh?" Gus said, reaching out and awkwardly, playfully knuckling his daughter in the ribs.

"Cut it out!" she snapped, her voice going thin and shrill. She whirled and banged the door in their faces.

Gus moved uneasily down the hall, trying to smile and saying, "Today is not feeling good, I guess."

Paul turned and saw Jimmy still standing, staring at the closed door. There was an odd thoughtful look on his face.

"Jimmy!" Paul said.

The boy seemed to shake himself, like a dog coming out of water. He turned from the door and came down the hall toward the staircase. Paul said, "Go on upstairs and unpack, Jim. I want to talk to Gus." The boy went up a few stairs, then stopped and turned when Paul said, "I'll have to be running along after that, Jim. Good luck."

"Thanks, Mr. Darmond."

Gus was silent on the way down to the front hall. He went into the living room. Doris had left. "Talk in here?"

"Fine, Gus. Sit down, will you?"

"Sure. I think he is a good boy, that Cheemee."

"This is something else. How has Teena acted lately?"

"Young girls, they get nerves, maybe. Not smiling much. Lot of dates. Popular, I think. Gets too thin and Anna worries about not eating."

"You haven't been keeping close track of her, have you?"

"No. Not too close. But why? Is a good girl. I . . . I do not watch enough, I guess. After Henry is killed, I . . ." He spread his hands in a helpless gesture and let them fall heavily to his thighs.

"Gus, she's in trouble."

Gus stared at him, wearing an apologetic smile, his eyes puzzled. The smile slowly faded away and the big hands closed into fists. "Trouble! You mean is having baby? You mean some boy is—" He began to stand up.

"Sit down, Gus. Worse trouble than that."

Gus sat down and the half-shy puzled smile returned. "Worse? Paul, what is worse? You make a joke, eh?"

"She's a drug addict, Gus."

The smile grew strained but it remained on his lips. "What big fool tell you that kind of lie, friend Paul?"

"Nobody told me. I could see it when I looked at her. Anybody who has had any experience with them could see it."

"No, Paul. Not my Teena. No. Good girl."

"Yes, Gus. It's the truth. There's a hell of a lot of it in the high schools. There's a lot of it among the girls. More than there ever was before. There's a lot of it coming into this section. They got on it and they have to get the money to keep buying it. Teena is a user, Gus. God knows what else she is if you haven't been keeping track of her."

Paul watched the man's face. He saw the look of stone that came over it. Gus got up and walked to the front windows and looked out across the porch into the street, his hands clasped behind him. Paul went over to him, put a hand lightly on his shoulder.

"Dirty," Gus said softly. "So dirty." He turned just enough so Paul could see his wet cheek. He raised one knotted fist. "I find who sells, and I kill."

"That doesn't help Teena."

"I know where the money comes from. I watch. Something is wrong in store. Same business, same prices, not so much money. This thing, it makes her steal from me. From her own pop, eh?"

"They'll do anything in the world to get the drug once they have the habit."

The old man turned around from the window, his face bleared with tears. "Tell me what I do, Paul. Tell me what I do now. My fault. All the time think of Henry. Henry is dead. Better I should be thinking of Teena." His voice broke. "What I do now, Paul?"

"I wouldn't want her turned over to the county authorities for the standard cure. The best place I know of is Shadowlawn Sanitarium. I know Dr. Foltz, the director. They do a good job out there. It's about fifteen miles out. It's expensive, Gus."

"Money anybody can have. Not daughters."

"She isn't going to go willingly. If she finds out what you're planning to do, she'll leave here. God knows where she'll go or what will happen to her before we can pick her up. Like all the rest of them, she won't talk about her connections until her nerves have had a chance to heal. Then she'll talk. And they'll clean up one more little group, and while they're cleaning it up, two more will be starting."

"I go up there with a strap. I make her talk, you bet anybody."

"Now settle down. You're not going to whip her. That won't do a damn bit of good. We'll try to keep this as quiet as possible. I'll let them know at the school, and maybe they can turn up a lead, the kids she was hanging around with. I'll check with Rowell and he can see that her friends are investigated."

"Not him, Paul. No. The shame!"

"I'll tell him to keep his mouth shut."

"Just like he talk with Bonny, maybe?"

"I'm sorry about that. I want to talk to her."

"Everything is go to hell, Paul."

"So we'll fix everything, Gus. Now make sure she doesn't leave the house. I'll phone Foltz and see if he wants to have somebody pick her up, or if he wants me to take her out there."

"Not from store."

"I'll go down the street and phone."

Paul went down the street and shut himself in a drug-store booth and phoned Dr. Foltz.

"Doctor, this is Paul Darmond. I've got a patient for you."

"Which kind this time, Paul?"

"Dope. Just a kid. A girl seventeen. Daughter of a friend of mine. I'll vouch for him as far as the fees are—"

"You don't have to say that. Is she willing?"

"I don't know. I doubt it. I happened to spot it just a few minutes ago."

"How does she look physically?"

"Pretty beat. Thin as a rail. Her name is Christine Varaki. Her father runs a market on Sampson Street."

"We're getting too many of them, Paul. It's rough on my people. They generally make at least one attempt to kill themselves the first week. Can you bring her out?"

"I guess so."

"Bring someone else along to help. Somebody husky. They look frail but they move fast. If she gets suspicious, she may try to grab the wheel."

"O.K. How long will she be out there? I want to tell her father."

"Depends on the strength of the habit and how run down she is. Tell him two months. That's a fair average. If he wants an estimate of how much it will cost, tell him twelve hundred. That ought to cover everything. She can't have visitors until she's been here two weeks. I'll mail him a form to fill out and sign and return. No, I can give it to you."

Gus was still sitting in the living room when he went back. He gave him the information.

"I'd like to get going as soon as I can, Gus. I have to take somebody with me. You want to come?"

"I . . . do not want to see what . . ."

"I understand. I ought to take somebody. Walter?"

"Better he should not know yet."

Paul remembered how Jimmy Dover had stood outside Teena's closed door. He said quickly, "How about the new boy? Is that all right with you?" It was an impulsive suggestion, he realized.

Gus frowned. "All right, I guess. Maybe she likes better some boy the same age, almost."

Jimmy Dover was sitting on his bed, staring out the window. He turned quickly as Paul came in. He blushed. "I was getting up my nerve to go downstairs, Mr. Darmond."

"Are you good at keeping things under your hat?"

"Yes, sir."

"I need your help, Jim. You noticed how strange Teena acted?"

"I sure did. I don't know. It bothered me."

"We've just found out she's a drug addict."

Dover whistled softly. "A junkie!"

"I'm taking her right away to a sanitarium outside of town. She might make quite a fuss. I'll have to drive and I may need somebody to hold her."

"Me? You want *me* to help?"

"Don't you think you can hold her?"

"Sure. But it just seemed . . ."

"You know where I parked the car. You go down to the car. I'm going to see if I can get her into some clothes and downstairs without a fuss. The trouble will start in the car, when we head the wrong way."

Paul walked down the second-floor hallway to Teena's door and rapped softly.

"Who is it? What do you want?"

"Paul Darmond, Teena. Police headquarters just located me here. They want me to bring you downtown."

"What for?"

"They've picked up a girl on a charge of theft. Saturday night. The girl claims she was with you. They want you to go down and make a statement."

"What's her name?"

"She hasn't given them her name."

"What does she look like?"

"They didn't say. She says she's a close friend of yours."

There was a long silence. "I'll get dressed and be down in a minute."

Paul went down and told Gus to go back to the market, to get out of sight. He was afraid Gus's face would be a giveaway.

Three minutes later Teena came slowly down the stairs, sliding her hand down the railing.

Chapter Ten

PAUL GOT BEHIND the wheel and Teena got in the middle. Jimmy got in and pulled the door shut.

"I think it's a girl I know named Ginny," Teena said.

Paul started the car. "A good friend?"

"I guess so."

"Were you with her Saturday night?"

"I'll tell them down there when I know who it is." Paul saw her give Jimmy an oblique glance. "Why're you coming too?"

"I got to go down there anyway. It saves a trip."

"You just got out, didn't you?"

"Yeah. Fresh out. Why?"

"I was just asking."

Paul turned off Sampson onto Crown Avenue and followed Crown east. He had to stop for a red light. Teena was staring straight ahead, her hands in her lap. Paul looked across her and gave Jimmy a quick nod. Jimmy casually moved his hands a bit closer to hers.

When the light changed, Paul turned right. For a moment Teena did not react, and then she straightened up. "Why're you going this way? Downtown is straight ahead."

"I have to make a stop," Paul said easily. "It isn't far out of the way."

She leaned back. "Oh."

She was silent while the blocks went by. They reached the city line and went on. She sat forward again. "There's something fishy about this. What's going on? Where are you taking me?"

"Just take it easy, Teena."

"What do you mean, take it easy?" Her voice was getting more shrill. "Where are you taking me?"

"To a place where they'll take care of you, where they'll make you well."

She sat still for at least three seconds and then exploded with a startling violence. Jimmy managed to clap his hands over her wrists. She drove her teeth down toward the back of his hand, but he managed to get his elbow under his chin in time. She was grunting and straining with the effort. She jabbed her left foot over toward the pedals and Jimmy hooked his big foot around her leg and yanked it back.

"Can you hold her?"

"I got her, Mr. Darmond."

"I won't go there! I won't stay!" he struggled again, so strongly that she nearly broke Jimmy's grasp, and then suddenly she lay back, panting. "I'm going to say you both got me in the back seat and attacked me. I'll swear it. On Bibles."

"Attack a junkie?" Jimmy said harshly. "I wouldn't touch you with a ten-foot pole. It makes me sick having to hold onto you."

"Easy, Jim," Paul said.

"Easy, hell. After this I'm going back and take a hot bath. Get a cure and maybe you'll be worth looking at. The way you are, kid, you stink!"

She crumpled forward, doubling over her imprisoned hands. Hard sobs shook her. Jimmy winked blandly at Paul across her thin shoulders. Suddenly he yelped as she bit his hand. He snatched it free and she leaned across him and grabbed for the door handle. He cuffed her and grabbed her wrists again. She called them both foul names for the next few miles, then became silent.

By the time they reached the sanitarium, there was no more resistance in her. They drove through wrought-iron gates and up a steep graveled road to the main building. People walked in twos and threes around the wide green lawns.

They took her to the receiving desk and the large woman there smiled and said, "Christine Varaki? Hello, dear."

Teena spat.

The woman's smile did not change. She picked up her phone and called an extension and said, "Dorothy? Are you ready for the Varaki girl?" She listened and hung up. "There'll be a nurse right down, dear. You look like the first thing you need is a good scrubbing and a shampoo."

"The first thing I need is a fix, Fatty."

"Mr. Darmond, the forms are in this envelope. Dr. Foltz said to tell you he's sorry he's tied up."

A solid-looking redheaded nurse with a pugnacious jaw came clacking down the echoing hall. She looked intently at Teena. "Golly, kid, they told me you were going to be a bad one. You got a lightweight habit. Come on."

Teena walked away with her with surprising docility. Only when she was forty feet down the hall did she look back. Her pallid face looked small, and she looked drab and thin beside the white confidence of the nurse.

They went back out to the car. When they turned out onto the highway Paul said, "Pretty rough, weren't you?"

"A guy did it for me once."

"Did what, Jim?"

"The first week I was up there. I was a hot charge. I was wired. Hard, man. One boy named Red took me off the strut. Caught me behind the laundry. Cuffed hell out of me. Proved to me I was a punk. A sixteen-year-old punk. It gives you a better look at yourself. I was doing the same thing. I hope it wasn't too much."

"I don't think it was."

They rode in silence for a few miles. Jimmy said, "Does the city bus come out this way?"

"There's a bus that comes out."

"I wonder if anybody'd kick if I came to see her, after they get her quieted down."

"I don't think they'd mind."

"Her friends are probably on the junk too. They wouldn't go within nine miles of that place. Somebody ought to go see her. Besides her family, I mean."

"Do you think it will help?"

"She was pretty, I bet."

"Very."

It wasn't until he parked in front of the store that Jimmy spoke again. He laughed and said, "It's crazy."

"What is?"

"That's the first girl I've had a chance to talk to in two years."

"This is going to be called a nervous breakdown, Jim."

"Sure. I understand."

They went in and Paul looked up Gus and told him there hadn't been any trouble, and gave him the papers. Gus said he had decided to tell Walter, and Walter could help him with the papers.

Paul knew that Walter would tell Doris. And Doris would, with a delightfully superior sense of her station, suck hungrily at this new horror, seeing not the tragedy of it, seeing it only as a distortion of her own environment, a new flaw that could be used to point up her own purity, using it as a little hammer to drive home more neatly the sharpened tacks that held firm the endless ribbon of her conversation. In a week the whole neighborhood would know what had happened.

Bonny was behind the counter, wearing a pale cardigan and gray slacks. There was no one nearby when he went over to her. She looked up into his face. "Yes?"

"I wonder if I could talk to you. I've got an errand that shouldn't take long. I'll be back in three quarters of an hour. Maybe you'd let me buy you a lunch?"

"You all move in at the same time, don't you?"

"It isn't like that, Bonny."

"What do you think it's like? Didn't they give you a badge you can show me?"

"I want to talk to you," he repeated stubbornly.

"Actually I don't have any choice, do I?"

"You do. But maybe you'd rather think you don't."

"Parlor psychiatry, Mr. Darmond."

He gave her a remote smile and went out to his car. Wentle was on one of his periodic tours of the big school. Paul waited in his office. There were dusty flags racked in the corners. There was a brooding picture of Lincoln. There were the hall sounds, feet shuffling between classes, babble, a high whinny of laughter.

Wentle came in, his mask of authority sagging into a puffy weariness. "Hello, Paul. Some days I think you should have my job. The problems seem to be about the same."

"No, thanks. I'm ulcer prone, Grover."

"You look like a man about to stir my ulcer up."

"This might, Grover. It's about the Varaki girl. Teena."

"Trouble? Do you want me to call her out of class?"

"She isn't here. She won't be in again this term, Grover. She's out at Shadowlawn, admitted today."

"Drugs?" Wentle asked, his eyes dull.

"Yes."

Grover Wentle got up and went over to the windows and looked down at the flat-roofed gym. "I should have guessed it last week. Such a change in attitude. I should have insisted that the nurse check her over. Disciplinary problem. Not like the girl."

He turned from the window. "Great God, Paul, it isn't enough that the classes are jammed, teachers hard to get. Five thousand and more students now. Just enough funds to handle bare maintenance. That charming time of life, adolescence. We want to give them outside activities. Teachers willing to supervise are damn rare. They don't get paid for it. My God, it's a hideous time of life when they run loose. Stuff that would sicken you. We found them using the auditorium, a bunch of them, as a big bedroom when they cut classes. That knifing two weeks ago. Running off pornography on the school mimeograph machine. They come from decent homes and get thrown into this millrace, and they think they have to conform. If they don't, they're labeled chicken. My God, Paul, it would strain you to the last inch to keep this place in line even without the drugs. A girl like Teena! I should have guessed it." He smiled sourly. "I'm getting pretty good at guessing it, Paul. I ought to—I'm getting enough practice. What's happened to kids? What's going wrong with the world?"

"It's a pendulum. Maybe it will swing back. Maybe it's already started to swing back."

"It better start soon, Paul. What can I do on this Varaki situation?"

"I want to know who she's been running around with lately."

Wentle placed his fingertips together, frowned. "I can call in a girl. Not a very attractive child, but she's been of help in the past."

Wentle had Miriam called out of one of her classes. She was a drab, owl-eyed girl with thin lips. She sat very straight in the chair beside Wentle's desk. Her attitude seemed to combine the arrogance of the reformer, the secret excitements of the informer.

"Can you tell us who Teena Varaki has been running around with, Miriam?"

Tongue flicked the thin lips, eyes narrowed behind lenses. "Messy people, Mr. Wentle. Ginny Delaney. She dropped out a while back. I guess Teena's boy friend is Hobart Fitzgerald. Fitz, they call him. He's always in trouble. Teena has been letting him . . . touch her in the halls." Miriam blushed delicately. "I just happened to see them a couple of times. Then there's Charles Derrain, the one they call Bucky. He cuts a lot of classes. He got thrown out of schools. Teena used to have nice friends. Now she's just like her new friends. Messy. Dirty, even. Like she didn't care any more. She never does her assignments any more and—"

"Thank you, Miriam," Wentle said softly.

The girl stood up. "Is she in trouble?"

"I'm afraid so, but that's just between us. She won't be back this semester. She's had a nervous breakdown."

Miriam sniffed. She stared sidelong at Paul and left, taking short quick steps.

After the door closed Wentle said, "The teachers are too busy to keep track, Paul. I know it's not doing Miriam any good to use her that way. She comes in and volunteers information."

"Can you give me the addresses that go with these names?"

"Of course. What will you do with them?"

"Turn them over to the proper people. This is extracurricular for me. I seem to keep my nose in other people's business."

"I'm glad you do."

"The worst part of it is telling their parents. I'm glad that doesn't come up often. You'll probably lose two more students, Grover."

"Seniors, too. And they probably won't be back. The parents won't blame themselves. They won't blame the kids. They'll blame the school. And me. It's a funny thing. When they're the children of a good solid happy marriage, they seem to stay out of trouble. I guess Teena is an exception to that rule."

"No, Grover. Her father married again. Her favorite brother was killed in March. Nobody has had much time for her since then. The house has been pretty gloomy for her, I think. It isn't going to be enough to cure the addiction. We've got to cure the emotional causes too, or she'll be back on it in a matter of weeks."

"I'll have those addresses looked up for you."

It was a quarter after one by the time he got back to the market. As he walked to the door he looked through the windows and saw Jana behind the cash register. Of all the people who lived and worked there, he realized he

knew the least—could guess the least—about Jana. He
knew only that his response to her was thoroughly male.
She had very little to say, yet in her silences there was
no deviousness, no subtleties. She had a look of sturdiness,
the uncomplicated woman. He saw her biting her lip and
slowly punching the register keys as she totaled an order.

As he reached the door Bonny came from the back of
the store toward the doorway, saying something to Jana
that he could not hear. Bonny looked at him with cool
recognition. She still wore the pale sweater, but she had
changed from slacks to a coarse-textured skirt.

"It took longer than I thought. How soon do you have
to be back?"

"I shouldn't stay away more than an hour."

Her attitude had changed. She was still cool, but there
was not so much animosity. He closed the car door on her
side and went around and got behind the wheel. She took
cigarettes out of her purse.

"I'm in a mood to get away from the neighborhood,
Bonny. There's a place on the Willow Falls road. You
can eat out back on a sort of terrace arrangement."

"All right."

The small coupé trudged sedately through traffic. Once
they were out of the city the hills were warm green with
June, and the air smelled of growth and damp change.
He looked straight ahead, yet in the corner of his eye
there was the image of her, the quiet face, the ripe liquid
copper of her hair, a burnishment against the green
changes of the countryside.

"It's good to get away from it," he said.

"I was trying to remember the last time I walked on a
country road," Bonny said. "God! Way back."

"I thought you were going to refuse to come."

He knew she turned toward him but he did not look
at her. There was a sudden warm deep sound in her
throat. Not a laugh. An almost sly token of amusement.
"I wasn't. I went to Gus. I said Rowell was more than
enough to take in one week. I asked him to tell you to
leave me alone. You know what he did? He grabbed me
by the shoulders. His eyes looked like when the gas is
turned low. He nearly shook me loose from my teeth. He
said I was his daughter and I was of his house, and I
would do what he said. He said I would go with you and
talk with you and stop making nonsense. It shocked me

and it almost scared me. After he settled down I began to get the pitch. I guess you're what is known as a friend of the family, Mr. Darmond."

"Gus is a very loyal guy. And I just . . . did him a favor."

"About Teena? He said something about Teena that I couldn't understand. What's going on there, anyway?"

"I'll tell you after we get some food. The place is just up the road. And call me Paul, will you, please?"

It was a small clean hillside restaurant, with bright colors, starched waitresses, checked tablecloths. There were four tables on the tiny terrace under the shade of vine-covered white latticework. The brook came down busily over brown rocks nearby.

As Paul walked behind Bonny to the farthest table he was aware of the way she walked, of the sway of skirt from the compact trimness of hips, how straight her back rose from the narrowness of the concave waist, how the sheaf of hair swung heavily as she turned to look back at him, one eyebrow raised in question as she gestured toward the table.

"Fine," he said, and held the chair for her.

She looked at the brook, and at the vines overhead, the blue sky showing through. "This *is* nice, Paul."

"I used to bring my wife here when we could afford it."

"You used to bring her?"

"She died over a year ago."

"I'm sorry. I didn't know that."

"There's no reason why you should have known it. I recommend their chicken pie. It has chicken in it."

"Imagine!" And again she made that warm sound in her throat. When her face was alive she was extraordinarily pretty. It was only when she retreated into espressionlessness that there was that look of hardness, of defiant glaze.

They ordered, and as they ate they talked of idle things, staying away from any serious subject as though they had carefully decided it in advance.

Chapter Eleven

THOMAS ARTHUR KARSHNER came up out of sleep, up out of dreams of thirty years ago. His bedroom glowed with the soft yellow of sun against the closed blinds, and he knew it was late. He lay quite still, retasting the vividness of the dream, knowing it would fade soon, wanting to hold it as long as he could. It was odd how, these past few years, the past was becoming more vivid. A sign of age, perhaps.

This dream had been of Caroline. Warm, young, alive, lovely. Not the thick fleshy body he had buried in '34, but the younger Caroline of those years right after the war. In the dream she had been looking for something in that New York apartment where they had lived. He had been helping her look. Yet she wouldn't tell him what it was they were searching for. Some precious thing that had been mislaid. The loss of it had frightened her in some obscure way.

The dream faded and the apartment was gone, and all Caroline's warmth dwindled to those few photographs, quite faded, of a slim woman in awkward outdated clothes. He lay and wondered what Caroline would think if she knew. How he would find the words to explain it to her, explain how it had come about.

You see, dear, it started in such a vague way. It wasn't as though there was any signpost. He'd been pointed out to me. There can be a certain fascination in evil. That was back when they were nailing so many of them for income-tax evasion when they couldn't get them on other counts, and it worried him. I didn't know that, at the same time, I was being pointed out to him, pointed out as a man who could make arithmetic do sly tricks. It started as a small service I performed for him. It amused me to do it. It gave me, with my friends, an amusing notoriety. You see, Caroline, he is not the sort of man to leave you alone if you can perform a service he wishes to buy. His affairs, even then, were vastly complicated. He wished to use me for other small services, all legal, of course. Yet he had to know he could trust me. And he is a very uncomplicated man in personal relationships. A trustworthy person is a person who does not dare to hurt you. He framed me with the casual efficiency with which a riding master saddles a horse. I was restive under the bit, and he soothed me with what he called "a yearly retainer." It soon became quite clear that he resented any work I did for others. My services for him became more and more extralegal, until at last the mere fact of having performed those services was as effective as the documentation of my private vices. For a long time I thought of myself as trapped. But I did not become truly trapped until I became aware of my comfort within the trap. My services were extralegal. In return I have received a silken existence, wine, steaks, brandy, cigars, and the touch of flesh when required, and the sense of power.

He permits me to take small liberties with him. To speak to him as an equal, almost. It is much the same way that a man might amuse himself by making a friend of his butler. I am the butler of his scattered household. I am the arranger, the smoother-out, the handler of funds, the taker of messages. I am required to devise little schemes that will make the household run more smoothly. It leaves him free to control policy. I keep his world in order.

I am very good at it, Caroline.

He can be at Las Vegas, Acapulco, Miami, New York, and know that while he is gone, things are conducted in an orderly fashion.

They call me the Judge, Caroline. I have cultivated a mild judicial manner, spiced with some tricks of force I have picked up from him. You would not recognize me.

I have profited, Caroline. In the past eight years he has acquired a passion for legitimate investment. I own blocks of stock in eight of his legitimate corporations. A chain of motels. Two large suburban shopping centers. A resort hotel. A small chain of liquor stores. A business block. Apartment houses.

Yet we continue most of our original sources of extralegal profit. Drugs, women, and gambling. A pretty trio. The marketing of thrills. On these mornings, Caroline,

I tell myself that I am old and tired, and aware of my own filth. Yet I know, with a certain melancholy, that during this day I will become comfortably aware of my own cleverness, that I will take a cold pride in my tact and my managerial abilities, that I shall find some small place of weakness during this day, and use the power I have by decree, and enjoy the use of that power.

You saw that same flaw, didn't you, Caroline? And that was what soured it all, at last. And he saw it too, and he has used it to his good advantage.

Karshner got out of bed slowly, standing like a plump red-faced child in his blue and white striped pajamas. In the bathroom he ran the brisk humming razor across his red face, the warm head biting off the white stubble with small crisp sounds. He lowered himself gruntingly into the hot tub, soaping the worn sagging body. He toweled himself harshly, brushed the white hair, clothed himself in white nylon underwear, in black silk socks, in handmade cordovan shoes, in a heavy creamy French linen shirt, in muted sapphire cuff links, in deep maroon knit tie, in the pale gray summer-weight suit. From the top of the bureau he took an alligator wallet, a small stack of change, a gold pen, and a gold key ring and placed them in the proper pockets.

Armed for the day, he phoned down to the desk. There had been two calls. He wrote the two phone numbers on the desk pad, then hung up and used the other telephone for the calls, first closing the small switch in the line that activated it. He paused before dialing the first number. It was not a good number to call from this phone. The world of electronics had made telephones unsafe. He held the phone in his hand, finger motionless in the first hole of the number, then shrugged and dialed the number. A woman answered.

"Karshner speaking," he said.

"Oh, sure. Hold on a sec."

The man came on the line. "Judge, I want to see you."

"That's very interesting. If you're eager I shall be finishing my breakfast in forty minutes. I shall be at the Walton Grill, last booth on the left. I can give you five minutes."

The booth was dark-paneled, the table linen sparkling white. The walls between the booths were low. The young girl poured his second cup of coffee. "Thank you, my dear," Karshner said, patting his lips with the heavy napkin. As the girl walked away he saw Brahko coming down the wide aisle between the booths wearing a distressing shirt. He resented having to talk to Brahko, resented any dealing with the more muscular division of the organization. Brahko was dark, and there was a handsome—in fact, almost a noble—look about the upper half of his face. But the chin faded meekly toward the collar and Brahko could cover his large yellow-white teeth only by distorting his lips oddly, like a man about to whistle. And, of course, he wore distressing shirts.

He sat down with a shade too much heartiness. "Good morning, Judge."

"Please don't phone me, Brahko. I don't like it. Who is that woman?"

"Don't get sweaty, Judge. She's all right. She's a good kid."

"Don't phone me. Is that clear?"

"I phoned you when I got this. It was in with the collection this morning. Take a look."

Karshner unfolded the piece of paper, aware that Brahko was watching his face carefully. He did not permit his expression to change as he read it. "The young man is astonishingly literate," Karshner said. "A pleasantly careful young man. You could learn from him, Brahko."

"I figured anything that might foul up the setup, you ought to know about, Judge."

Karshner continued as though he had not been interrupted. "A careful young man up to a point. Aiding the young girl out of her difficulties yesterday was astonishingly stupid. I am afraid he is erratic. I was aware of that when he insisted on the very melodramatic way of enlisting the services of his accomplice. Yet he's been quite effective."

"Can you do anything?"

Karshner lit a corner of the note and placed it in the glass ash tray. When it had burned away, he puddled the fragments with the end of the burned match.

"You have informed me, Brahko."

"Sure, but are you going to *do* anything?"

"It is unfortunate that one of your . . . ultimate consumers should be a member of the same household. It could attract unwelcome attention. The young man is quite correct about that. However, his proposed solution is as devious and erratic as his method of acquiring the services of the butcher."

"I don't get it, Judge."

"His own act imperils the operation to a greater extent than the child's addiction. I believe we must consider new methods of wholesale distribution."

"What are you going to *do ?*"

"Should the child be cured, Brahko, she will at some point report that our young man took care of her needs. She will also report her other source or sources, but that need not concern us. What does concern us is that our young man is going to receive some unwelcome attention when the child becomes penitent."

Brahko nodded slowly. "I get it. He shouldn't have got her a fix."

"Correct. By doing so, he impaired his value to us, and rendered his own suggestion invalid. The action we take must be more direct. I suspect that it is a matter that we can turn over to Guillermo for necessary action."

Brahko stared at him. "Say, like it says in the note, the kid is only seventeen."

"I don't believe that has deterred Guillermo's operations in the past. I believe you should contact him, Brahko. She should be quite pliable. Tell him that it will be wise to hand her over to one of the more distant establishments. Norfolk, Memphis, Jacksonville. And he should induce her to leave a parting message. A plaintive little note. 'Do not try to bring me back.' Guillermo knows the procedure. And perhaps a letter from her mailed from some distant point."

"She's pretty young."

"Brahko, the softness of your heart astonishes me. Or is it that you hate to lose one of your consumers?"

"Maybe you ought to check before you make it an order, Judge."

Karshner sat very still for a moment. He looked at Brahko in utter silence until the man shifted uneasily and said, "I just meant that maybe there'd be some other way of—"

"You aren't handling yourself well, Brahko. The phone call. The unknown woman. Your obvious nervousness. You make me wonder how adequately you are performing."

"Judge, I was just—"

"See Guillermo today, Brahko. That's all."

Brahko stood up. Karshner watched him leave, and then signaled to the girl to bring more coffee. He bit the end from his first cigar of the day. He wondered what the young Varaki girl was like, and then forced that thought from his mind. It was much safer to think of them as factors in some vast complicated equation. That young man, Lockter, could be removed just as readily, and no damage done. If they took him in and he talked for ten days to police stenographers, he could not tell them anything that could be construed as evidence against anyone higher up in the organization. Lockter could topple the peddlers, but there were always peddlers. It was the old immutable cycle of supply and demand. If the supply channels collapsed, demand pressure would bump the price back up again to the place where new peddlers would accept the risk.

Guillermo's people would handle the child correctly, using the drug the way you entice a kitten with a scrap tied to the end of a string. He finished his third cup of coffee and wished, with a certain regret, that he had told Brahko that he would contact Guillermo himself. That would have given him a chance, while speaking to Guillermo, to indicate that a small favor would be appreciated. It had been quite a long time now. Longer than ever before.

There was, of course, the problem of getting word to Lockter. A strange young man. A strange glitter about him, like knife blades. A flawed young man. Too fond of intrigue for the sake of intrigue. He should be told that it was out of his hands, and he should be informed that his procuring of the drug for the child was astonishingly stupid. Given that little morsel, Rowell would enjoy long talks with Lockter.

He remembered the last time he had spoken to Rowell. The memory made his cheeks burn dully. Rowell had elbowed him into a corner of a hotel lobby, out of sight behind the public phone booths.

"Patties up, Judge."

"Take your hands off me!"

"Now, Judge," Rowell had said soothingly, and made of the business of searching him a brutal game, roughing him up with ease of long practice, elbow under the chin to click the teeth sharply, hard knee bruising the thigh, hand thudding hard over the kidneys, so that Karshner's hat had fallen to the dusty floor, and his eyes had filled with tears, and he gagged for breath.

"You can't do this to me!"

"Why, I just did, Judge. You want special treatment when I brace you? You figure you're better than any little punk in your organization? You look just the same to me, Judge. Why don't you sue me or something? Upstanding citizen assaulted by police brutality. Why don't you tell me you'll see that my badge is lifted or something? Isn't that the usual line? Better pick up your hat, Judge."

He had started to pick it up, and then turned around so that he wouldn't be facing away from Rowell. He picked up his hat, brushed it on his sleeve, and hurried down the steps to the side door of the hotel followed by Rowell's laughter. The incident had made him think of schoolyards of long ago. Tommy Karshner crying helplessly. They used to get him in a circle and push him back and forth until he fell.

The Judge left his usual generous tip and got up from the booth. It was nearly noon. He decided to take a short walk to settle his heavy breakfast, and then drop in his offices, the offices of the Johnston Service and Development Corporation, check the mail, and then go over to the sedate Johnston Athletic Club for prelunch cocktails and perhaps a few hands of bridge. Another hour at the office in midafternoon should be enough to take care of the routine. As he walked he again felt a lingering regret that he had not arranged to contact Guillermo himself. It involved a slight loss of dignity to go to Guillermo with only that one obvious reason. And suddenly he realized that one of Guillermo's people might be ideal to use to contact Lockter and give him the word. The two functions of informing Lockter and setting up the young lady's trip might be best handled simultaneously. It involved fewer contacts. He lengthened his stride a bit and compressed his stomach muscles and squinted ahead into the June sunshine.

Chapter Twelve

OVER COFFEE Paul said, with that sudden grin that changed his face, "They call me the Preacher."

"I know," Bonny said. "I'm braced."

"For what?"

"A rehash of my duty to myself, to God, my country, and the Varakis."

"I meddle, Bonny. I get curious about people. I get most curious about them when their masks don't fit well."

"Masks?"

"You make me think of a social lassy trying to play a cheap chippy in a B movie. When you forget the act, you begin to come through better."

"The real me? Goodness gracious!"

"How much college did you have?"

"Three years. Why?"

"Dreams of your name in lights, maybe?"

"You're sharper than you look. Yes. And was told I was talented."

"And you were what is uncommonly known as a good girl?"

She looked down at her hand, clenched in her lap.

"A very good girl," she said. "Virginal at nineteen. Dreams of future bliss. It was going to be like floating on fattest pink clouds, when it finally happened. Turned out to be a pretty functional operation. Very sweaty affair, you know."

"Trying to shock me, Bonny?"

"Not particularly."

"Maybe you are. And that would be part of it, too."

"Part of what?"

"A result of that tremendous, ridiculous burden of guilt you're staggering around with."

She made herself look at him. "Guilt? That's an interesting idea. Hmm. Nice plot line."

"Shock me. Shut me out. Any defense you can find. The next step will be to make a large pass. To prove to yourself that you're a tramp at heart and you've proved it and you're going to keep on being one, so there."

"Please shut up!"

"I'm going to, Bonny. But first I'm going to tell you a story. A true one. There was a man of thirty in Johnston who lived with his mother. He had an IQ of about seventy, I'd guess. Just a big dumb harmless guy who parked cars for a living. Drove well, too. Most feeble-minded people do. Didn't drink or smoke. Some of his buddies got him drunk one day. For a gag. He went home reeling, got mad at his mother for objection, and took a punch at her. Just one punch. It happened to kill her. There were enough extenuation circumstances so that he got a short-term manslaughter rap. He went to prison and began to drive the authorities nuts. They couldn't figure out where he was getting it. They watched him. But every few days he'd really tie one on. Reel and stumble around and pass out. Finally some genius gave him a balloon test. Not a damn bit of alcohol in his system. Guilt, Bonny. Drunk on guilt. Labeling himself as a drunk."

She stared at him. "It's not that way. I know what I am. I know damn well what I am."

"No. You don't know what you are. You've selected an arbitrary label. Tramp. I just don't think it's accurate."

"It's not the real me? I see. Actually, I'm the reincarnation of Joan of Arc. I'm full of a suppressed desire to walk barefoot through dewy fields and talk with the birds."

"If your self-classification was accurate, Bonny, your act would have more unity. Now it's an off-and-on deal."

"Maybe we aren't getting basic enough, Paul. Maybe there's a better question—one that I can ask you. What difference does it make? What's your angle? Maybe it's an act, maybe it isn't. So what?"

"If it's an act, Bonny, then you have to keep your mind on it, and keep your attention away from other people. If it's an act, you're rolling in it, enjoying the pathos and tragedy. It's damn selfish."

"You're out of line. I'm not standing still for that kind of critique.'

She stood up. He looked at her with an entirely different expression. "Sit down, Bonny."

"Listen, I—"

"Sit down. I wasn't concerned with your welfare. Teena adored Henry. He's gone. What was left for her? A grieving old man. A bewildered young wife. A pregnant nag. A sour brother. Old Anna. Vern Lockter. And you. But you were too busy with yourself to see loneliness even, much less try to do anything. So you share it with the rest of them. A new load of guilt, Bonny. I think if you'd tried to understand her situation and make a friend of her after Henry was killed, I wouldn't have had to take her to a sanitarium this morning for a cure for drug addiction. You were too damn wound up in your own petty **little** torment to see a real hell shaping up right in front of you. And if Teena comes back into an unchanged household, Bonny, that cure is going to be only temporary. I want you there, and I want you straightened out and through playing your stupid game with yourself when she gets out. And while she's away, you can practice on the new kid, Jimmy Dover. He's a good kid, but he's going to need some kind of prop. Somebody to help hold him up. Don't flatter yourself that I'm fingering your little illusions because I'm trying to do you good. I'm trying to help Teena because she needs it more than you do or ever will."

When he stopped talking the brook noise seemed too loud. It made a sound in her ears like the sound heard before fainting. She saw herself, for one long shattering moment, with cruel objectivity. Saw all the self-pity, the blinded selfishness, the self-dramatization. Those hours Friday when she had sat alone in her room and heard the bus sounds had seemed so filled with a torment that was bittersweet. It had been, she saw, merely an exercise in ego, another scene in the long drama of self.

"Dear God," she said softly.

"We better leave," he said.

He drove a mile farther along the road and pulled off where the shoulder was wide. "I should get back," she said.

"That walk in the country you talked about might help a bit. Monday is slow, isn't it? Jana can handle it."

She got out dutifully, still feeling numbed and shocked. There was a path that curved up and around the shoulder of a small hill. She walked ahead of him on the narrow path. Beyond the hill was a jumbled pile of dull gray glacial rocks, bushel-sized and sun-warmed. She sat on one. He gave her a cigarette and then sat on the moist ground, his back against the rock she sat on. She looked at the whorl of hair at the crown of his head, at the gray hairs in the sunlight. The highway was not in sight. There was a distant farm, some fence rows of trees.

"Poor damn kid," she said. "I've seen them. I could have been one, I guess. I tried it once. I was sick for days from it. An allergy, I guess."

"You were sort of trying to . . . blot yourself out, weren't you?"

"I guess so. Lose identity. Lose everything."

"That can be a strong compulsion."

"Henry brought me out of it, even when I didn't want to come out of it. I didn't want the pain of being alive and having to think and know."

"What started it?"

"A guy. I looked at him and I didn't see what he was. I saw what I wanted him to be. And he wasn't. He had no more thought of marrying me than of flying like a big bird. But don't think I went around bleeding on account of that. I got him out of my system, but in the process I got myself all mixed up."

"Teena won't talk yet. She will, eventually. I keep wondering how much guilt is mixed up with other things. How about Vern Locker? Do you think he could have helped push her over the edge?"

"I don't know. I know the type. A very sharp apple. Very aware of himself. I saw the way he looked at me at first and I waited for the pass. It didn't come, for some reason. Offhand, I'd say no. But that's only a hunch. I mean if he didn't want to get tied up with me in any way, I guess it would have been more from caution than anything else. I'm his type, I'd imagine. If it was caution, that would go double with Teena, wouldn't it? But isn't he one of your wards? How come the suspicions, Paul?"

"I just have a feeling it's not working out. Maybe his mask doesn't quite fit, either."

"Don't start that again," she said mildly.

"Still sore?"

"No, Paul. But I want to think. I want to do an awful lot of thinking. Because I can sense all the resistance I have to that guilt-mask idea of yours. Too much resentment. So much that maybe it's true. And I want to think it out and see if it is true."

"And if it is?"

"Maybe you've finished what Henry started. A very thankless process of putting the girl back on her own two legs. But no matter what, there are still a lot of bad dreams you can't forget."

"Don't enjoy thinking of how bad the dreams are."

"You know too damn much, Paul."

"I don't know enough. Yet."

She stood up and moved a bit away from the rock so she could look down at him. She saw the way he looked up at her, and saw the way his mouth changed in that first look of awareness of her as something desirable. It was something she did not want to see, particularly at that time, especially from Paul Darmond. To cover her own momentary confusion she awkwardly put her hand out to help him up and said, "Rise and shine, you parlor philosopher. I've got to go to work."

His hand was hard and warm, and she made a mock show of tugging him to his feet. He stood and he did not release her hand. With his other hand he cautiously, gingerly touched the bright sheaf of her hair, smoothing it tenderly back from her temple, cupping then her cheek warmly with the hand's hardness, bending and kissing her lips while she stood, making no sign of movement, stood with a stillness all about her and in her heart.

And, with sudden self-hate, with a kind of tortured despair, she pulled at him and thrust her body insolently against him and widened her lips, burlesquing desire and feeling only a deadness within herself. He pushed her away and his eyes had gone narrow. His hand came up and she stood, awaiting the blow. He held his hand poised for a moment, then scrubbed the back of it against his mouth. She watched his anger go away quickly.

"Why did you do that?" he asked in a quiet voice.

"Isn't that the reaction you wanted?" Her anger came quickly, shaking her. "You, you're so goddamn brilliant! What do you want? something winsome? Should I blush and simper, for God's sake? What difference does it make to me? Take anything you want. The merchandise is free. This is a nice handy place. If you want something quick and al fresco I'll be glad to—"

She didn't hear the slap. It came as a hard red explosion inside her head. She saw the flick of his hand. She stumbled sideways and caught herself. The sharp sting made her eyes water and she looked at him, shocked. He stood, calm and tired-looking, watching her with a certain remote curiosity.

She ran by him, ran down the path toward the road. As she reached the road she slowed down. She stood still for a moment and then crossed and got into the car. She looked out at the fields on that side of the road. She heard the scuff of his shoe on asphalt. The door latch clicked and the car tilted a bit under his weight. The car door chunked shut. She saw his hand as he reached across her knees and punched the glove-compartment button with his finger. It fell open and she saw the blue and white of the box of tissue in there.

She reached in and took several and shut the glove compartment. He started the motor and said, "Cry or don't cry. But don't sit there and sniffle."

"Shut up."

The tires squeaked as he U-turned on the narrow road. He spoke in a quiet conversational tone. "I've been trying to figure it out. I mean the original kiss. I suppose part of it is due to the body making its normal demands. I haven't touched a woman since Betty died. And another part is due to the way your hair looked in the sun. That's a fine color with gray eyes. You're a handsome woman."

"Dig, dig, dig. Poke and pry. Why do you have to take everything apart? And why all the damn fuss about a kiss, anyway?"

"It was an improbable act, that's all. It startled me."

"Good God!"

"It was perhaps subject to misinterpretation."

"The Preacher!"

"The Preacher. That's right. Sociology with overtones. I'm of the opinion, Bonny, that's it's all just a mass application of moral codes that are constantly in a state of flux. But in any time, in any race, there are certain standards. Humility, decency, generosity. We all have some of that in varying amounts. And we've all got the reverse side of the coin, too. Fear, loneliness, evil."

She dropped the balled tissue out the window. "How much of those first three things does Rowell have?"

"A good amount, actually. He had just oversimplified his thinking. There's the good guys and the bad guys. In his book you're one of the bad guys, Bonny. If you should go for a walk in the evening alone, he might very possibly pick you up for soliciting. And they'd find a five-dollar bill in your purse with the corner torn off, and one of his boys would swear that he gave it to you. And it wouldn't bother him a bit that it was faked. You're one of the bad guys, so anything goes. Could you take that?"

She hunched her shoulders. The day suddenly seemed cold. "I don't know. I don't know if I could take that."

"He thinks I'm some kind of a crackpot. Once a crook, always a crook. He says he can almost tell them by looking at them. Like all successful cops, he has a group of informants. He despises them. He shakes and gouges and bullies the information out of them. But they have a grudging respect for him because he never betrays a source, and never breaks his word, once it's given."

"And he's kind to dogs and children," Bonny said bitterly.

"He's a working cop. He's a club society uses to protect itself. A weapon?"

"And it's all right with you if he goes around framing people? If he arrested me the way you said?"

"I'd go over his head and get you out of it."

"Then be careful crossing streets, Paul. Because I couldn't take that."

"Yesterday you couldn't. Tomorrow you can."

"Is that your handiwork?"

"Isn't it?"

"Just leave me alone, Paul. Just leave me alone."

He parked in front of the market and turned so that he faced her, one arm resting along the back of the seat.

"Bonny, I act more confident than I feel. It's a habit, I guess. I've tried to act as though slapping you across the chops was excusable. It wasn't. I'm very sorry."

"It's all right. I needed it."

"You didn't need it, Bonny. I'd like to see you . . . nonprofessionally."

"Remember the old joke, Paul? Your profession or mine?"

"Is that an answer?"

"I'd like to see you. I'd like to go out there again."

When she was in the market she turned and looked back. He was just starting the car. He grinned. She raised her hand half timidly.

Jana said, "Gee, I'm glad you're back."

"Give me a minute to change, huh?"

Bonny went up to her third-floor room and closed the door and leaned against the closed door for a moment. There was no sense to it. It was absurd that at this moment she should feel more alive, more vibrantly alive than at any time in too many years. Steady on, girl. Easy, there. Don't start hunting that old myth again, because it always drops you hard.

Chapter Thirteen

THE PLACE was called Artie's Dayroom, and, except for the fish, it was a very ordinary place. It was a single narrow room with a sturdy dark bar, six plywood booths, twelve unanchored bar stools, a vast turbulent jukebox, framed licenses, a framed dollar bill, a simple liquor stock, a large beer trade . . . and the fish.

Where there had once been the traditional mirror of the back bar, Artie had a built-in tank installed, indirectly lighted, and stocked with tropical fish that were like mobile costume jewelry and bits of gay ribbon darting and drifting among their weeds, snails, and castles. Artie was a pork-bellied leathery man with vague eyes and a high-pitched voice. When trade was slack he watched the fish. Good business came from the loners. The ones who would claim a stool and drink steadily and watch the fish. More restful than TV, Artie said. Vern could see what he meant. He had been in the bar since nine, waiting for the slow minutes to pass until ten o'clock. Monday-night business was slow. A bar-stool couple sat with their thighs touching, murmuring, their noses an inch apart, their eyes looking drowned. Two loners watched the fish. A habitue of the place, Rita, fed coins to the jukebox and jiggled slowly in front of it, snapping her fingers. She had the puffed, forgotten face of the alcoholic.

The music stopped and she came over to her glass, beside Vern's. She took two long swallows and said leaning against Vern's arm and shoulder, "Din that one get you, Vern? Din that send you?"

"I wasn't listening."

"You just got no ear, baby. No ear 'tall. My God, that one's bedroom music, Vern." She turned and yelled down the bar, "Gimme another drink and some nickels, Artie."

The soft pressure was removed from Vern's arm. She

112

got her fresh drink and the nickels and went back to the machine, bending over to study the labels in her near-sighted way.

Vern took another sip of his drink. He turned and looked through the glass of the door. The street gleamed wet in the night rain, and green neon across the street was reflected against the shiny black. It was a night to nurse a drink. It was a night to sit and feel a funny knot in your middle. This thing had, all at one, got out of hand. He sat relaxed on the stool. He could hear Rita, behind him, snapping her fingers over the music beat. He thought of the packed jars, nested in the tamped earth.

At three minutes of ten Vern picked up his change, leaving half a buck for Artie, and said, "See you."

"Folding early, kid?" Artie asked.

"Long day," Vern said. He made himself move slowly. He felt all knotted up inside. The rain had stopped. He turned right and walked in the direction he had been told, thinking of how it could be a setup, of how it could be a nice neat way of protecting the list of peddlers, of how he could be meat for the quick identifying spotlight and the short burst that would tear him apart inside. But they didn't like it rough any more. Now things were legitimate, with the syndicates settling disputes over area and territory. If they decided you were a handicap, it was a lot easier to wire your ankles to a cement block and put you in forty feet of water.

Out of the corner of his left eye he saw the black gleam of the car hood. He didn't turn. The voice said, "Lockter!"

He turned then and crossed over to the car door. The front door of the sedan opened. No interior lights went on and he noted that and guessed they had been dis-connected. The dash glowed faintly green. The Judge was behind the wheel. Locker realized he'd never seen the Judge driving a car before.

He got in and pulled the door shut. He was aware of somebody behind him in the back seat, and as the Judge drove on, Vern started to turn to look back.

"Eyes front," the Judge said softly.

"Sure." Vern told himself that this was no time to gabble. Let them do the talking. Act calm. He lit a cigarette. They turned into a run-down residential sec-

tion where the street lights were widely spaced, and
parked where it was dark. The Judge turned off the lights,
left the motor on. It was barely audible.

Vern made his hand slow as he lifted the cigarette to
his lips. He took a deep drag, snapped the butt out the
wing window toward the unseen sidewalk. He realized
then it was a one-way street, and that no car could head
toward them, throw headlight beams into the dark sedan.

"Have a busy day, Lockter?" the Judge asked.

"I certainly did."

"You started out with that idiotic note."

"O.K. I was wrong. I admit that."

"Not so much wrong as stupid. Say it."

"I was stupid."

"How did the contact go?"

"I came back after my second delivery. There was a
guy hanging around. He came over to the truck when
I got out. He said he'd been looking for the Varaki kid.
He said she wasn't in school. He'd checked that. I said
she was up in her room. He said I should go make some
deal with her to get her out of the house tonight. I said
I could do that all right. I asked him what the score was.
He said she was going on a trip. He said he'd hang around
until I set it up with her and gave him the word. He
gave me an address to take her to, about nine tonight.
I went in the house and she wasn't there. I couldn't figure
it out. The old man was acting funny. So funny I didn't
want to get too nosy. Finally I figured that Doris charac-
ter was the one to ask. She knows everything that goes
on. She tells me, in a sort of nasty way, that Teena had
had a nervous breakdown and she's in a sanitarium. The
new kid is there. Dover. I finally figured it out that Dover
had been brought around by Darmond and that Darmond spotted her and did something about it right away.
He always has his nose in other people's business. So I
went down and saw that guy again and told him. Then
he came back about five and told me how I should meet
you."

The Judge said softly, "Mr. Darmond had a busy day.
Rowell had some of his people pick up the kids the
Varaki girl ran around with. One of the boys implicated
two pushers. The Varaki girl is in a private sanitarium.
Shadowlawn. Run by Foltz. I think, Lockter, you can
read what is written on the wall."

"I guess so. The old cycle. When the cure starts to take she'll get religion. Then she'll say I got her some stuff. Then they'll land on me. I'll do more time."

"They'll want to know where you got it."

"So I tag one of the pushers they've already picked up."

"And that's all?"

"Sure. Why should I give them more than that?"

"Because you happen to possess information that can be traded, Lockter, for personal freedom. Understand, it won't do any more than inconvenience us. But we don't like being inconvenienced. The stuff is rolling in smoothly, and will keep on coming in smoothly. To guarantee continuity of supply, we can't cut our standing order. And if we can't distribute, that means a lot of money tied up in stocks that won't move until a new distribution setup is arranged.'

"I . . . see what you mean. If you want me to take a fall, O.K. But she won't talk for maybe ten days, two weeks. I could run."

"We don't like that either."

Vern heard his own voice go shrill. "Well, what the hell do you want me to do?"

He half heard a shifting behind him, and he managed not to glance back in his sudden panic.

"Don't get nervous, Vern," the Judge said softly.

"I'm not nervous."

"You should be, Vern. We talked about you today. We can't risk trying to take that girl out of Shadowlawn. It could be done, perhaps, but it isn't a good gamble. We'd be very stupid to trust you, Vern, because we haven't got enough of a handle on you. You're too erratic to be trusted, in any case. Then we discussed killing you. That could be done with minimal risk. I'm sure you can see that."

"Now wait, I . . ."

"But that would leave your friend Sussen in possession of as much inconvenient information as you have. We could make your death look accidental. But two fatal accidents compound risk. I assure you, we are not being melodramatic. This is a matter of business. We realize now that your rather dramatic distribution system was a mistake. We should have kept our . . . normal methods. Now this will be an intelligence test, Lockter. What do you think we would like you to do?"

"My God, I don't—"

"Think, Vern. Think hard."

Vern lit a cigarette, noting that his hands shook. The back of his neck felt cool. He did not like the way the Judge had made him feel young, stupid, unimportant. He thought back over the bewildering conversation. He said, thinking aloud, "You think you need more of a handle on me. And you think Stussen isn't of any use any more on account of . . . I guess you've decided to give up the delivery system."

"Correct. You're doing splendidly."

"Then I guess maybe you want me to kill Rick Stussen."

"There's a certain promise to you, son. Under stress you can think quite constructively. You do that and then we'll be happy to trust you to take a fall for supplying the girl and not attempt a trade. I would say that in view of your previous record, three years would be a reasonable sentence. Three years and a guarantee of employment when you are released. If you bungle the killing, no information you can give them will keep you from at least a life sentence. We, of course, would like to have evidence of premeditation."

"What do you mean?"

The Judge turned on the dash lights, took a small notebook and a pencil from his pocket "I'll dictate and you write, Vern. I think if you lean close to the dash lights, you can see well enough."

"Look, I don't—"

"Come now, Vern. This is just good procedure. Date it, please, at the top. Go ahead. That's fine. The salutation should be—let me see now . . . 'Darling baby.' That's certainly anonymous enough. Here's the message. 'Maybe I'm wrong, but I meant what I said last night about that Rick Stussen. He's too damn dumb to live. Don't worry about me. I'm going to figure some way to kill him so they'll never catch me. Burn this note, baby. I trust you. It would look like hell in court, wouldn't it? Ha-ha! Same place, same time tomorrow night, baby. All my love.' Now sigh it 'Vern.' Thank you, son." The pad was taken out of his hand. The Judge examined it. "Glad you didn't try to disguise your handwriting. You gave us a sample this morning, you know."

Vern felt a coldness inside him. One thing was perfectly obvious: With that note in existence, he would not dare kill Stussen. They couldn't trap him that way. So pretend agreement, and make plans, and run like hell. Run to where they'd never find him. With that decision made, confidence began to seep back into him.

"Now, Vern," said the Judge, "let us just review your possible courses of action. One, you kill Stussen skillfully. Then you are picked up for supplying heroin to the Varaki girl and this note in our files guarantees your loyalty to us, because if you talk, the note will be sent to the authorities and the Stussen affair will be reopened. Two, you bungle the Stussen killing and you are picked up for it. You will still keep silent because this note, showing premeditation, will guarantee your electrocution. Three, you try to run for it. One of our people will kill Stussen and we will send the note in and let the authorities help us run you down. No matter who finds you first, our people or the law, you will quite certainly die. I think we can safely say, Vern, in the vernacular, that this note wraps you up."

"If I don't bungle it, and do my time without talking, do I get the note back?"

"I'm sorry, my boy. There's no statute of limitations on murder. The note will be kept in a safe place. It could be considered a form of contract for your future services. A business asset."

Vern thought of all the implications for three long seconds and then, moving very quickly, stabbed his hand out at the pocket where the Judge had placed the notebook. His fingertips barely touched the fabric when he was slugged from behind, rapped sharply over the left ear. It was done skillfully He spiraled down through grayness to the very edge of unconsciousness and then come slowly back up to the real world of the car and the dim dash lights and the darkness. He bent forward, his hand cupping the throbbing place over his ear.

"We'll let you out here, Vern," the Judge said. "Today is Monday. Make this week's deliveries. You'll have to take care of Stussen before next Monday. Monday morning leave the collection in the usual place. But there'll be no more deliveries, of course. That means you'll have between now and next Saturday night to plan how you'll arrange the matter of Stussen. It should occur Saturday night or Sunday."

"Want to tell me exactly when, where, and how?" Vern asked bitterly.

"I've never cared a great deal for sarcasm," the Judge said.

Vern got out of the car. It rolled smoothly away and, forty yards up the street, the Judge turned the lights on. Vern walked for a little way, and then he was sick. He supported himself with one hand against a tree. He wiped his lips with his handkerchief and threw it over a hedge into a small yard. His heels made empty sounds in the street. It was always the same. One slip, one impulse, and they came in on you. Impulse to fix the kid up. Impulse to take over and suggest a course of action. One slip and they had you. No more the soft-stepping, the slick cat-foot silences, the secret ways. No more. The money there, tamped in dirt. No good. Paper. Use it and all the Rowells moved in. Where did you get it? How did you get it? No more escape.

Unless . . .

He stopped. The city night was like soft movement around him. Unless. And that was the one thing that would make the note valueless. He wondered why he had forgotten. Someone had to kill Stussen violently and in anger and with an utter carelessness of consequence, and with a perfect willingness to confess the crime. The old man had the shoulder meat from hoisting ten thousand crates of food, ten thousand sides of beef. The old man had anger. Anger now at what had happened to Teena. Anger at what could happen to Jana. Jana, unused wife, feeling the shifting subtle torment of the body's demands, while the old man dreamed of a lost son and now would dream of a daughter equally lost. Jana, moving in ancient instinctual patterns, most vulnerable because of that lingering Old World tradition of submission. And he sensed how it could be done.

Chapter Fourteen

JANA HEARD a faint creak on the staircase. Gus, beside her, filled the warm still air of the room with harsh metronomic snores. She heard a sound of water running. She turned her head and looked at the luminous dial of the bedside clock. A little after twelve. That would be Vern, the last one in. All in, now. Except for Teena. Teena away in some strange place. In a white bed in a white place with white lights in the halls, and a smell of sterilizing.

The nights were long. Unbearably long. It seemed impossible to exhaust the stubborn body. She thought longingly of the harvest times. The roar of the binder and the prickling of dust and chaff on sweaty faces. And working as hard as a man through the long hot days until your back was full of bitter wires, and the hard bed became as deep and soft as clouds, and morning came the instant you closed your eyes.

She remembered the barn dances, the sturdy stompings, the hard twang and scrape of the music, the nasal chant, the prance and bounce and the hard locked arms, and the quick, frank, stirring touches during the fast music beat. It had all happened in a faraway world where everything looked golden. The barn lights, the fields, the folded glow of the sun. She remembered the shy boy from down the road. Peter. The October day on the fresh spread hay in the unused box stall they had lost all shyness. After that they were together whenever they could manage it. All in a lost golden world. They had never seemed to think of talk about anything beyond the times they could be together. And then it had all ended that terrible day in August. That picnic day.

Peter had driven the two of them out there in his family's pickup truck. Vast sandwiches, dandelion wine, and nearly half of a not quite stale chocolate cake. They'd walked from the pickup carrying the picnic lunch down to their place—a steep cut in the bank with a soft flat bed of moss and grass. The cut angled back so that when they were at the very end of it they could not see the lake at all, nor could they be seen by anyone unless that person looked directly down at them, a project that would be considerable hampered by thorn bushes.

With the sun directly overhead so that it shone down on the soft green bed and on them, warmly, they had made love for quite a long time and then, vastly hungry, had eaten every scrap of the food. The sun no longer came into the cut and they drank the wine and then made love in the green shadows. Then he had pulled on his swimming trunks and gone out of the cut and she had lain back, feeling the wine in her, feeling the prickle of the grass against her, feeling the contentment and the drifting sweet exhaustion. She had thought she heard him call and she remembered that she had smiled. At last, yawning, she had put on her own suit and gone out. He was not there. He was always playing jokes. She called him, guessing that he had come out of the water and hidden himself. He wouldn't come out. She called him and then she sulked and she called that she was going to drive the truck home and leave him. She grew angry and while she was angry the sun moved behind a cloud in the west. The blue lake slowly turned gray and the wind made it choppy. The wind was cool and she hugged herself, shivering. The day was suddenly lonely, cold and empty, and she was no longer angry, but frightened as she looked at the grayness of water.

They found him when dawn was beginning to make the harsh floodlights look pale. She had refused to leave. She sat on the hill wrapped in the blanket with her father's hand tight on her shoulder, watching the slow movements of the boat lights. She saw how it would be for him down there, with his drowned hair, and his thin tanned face, and the lean strong body that had loved hers.

They hooked his flesh at dawn and brought him up, and some of the boats came in and the others headed down the lake, back to their home docks.

She went down the hill with her father's arm around her, and looked at him before they carried him up the hill to the county ambulance. She thought he would look frightened, or as if he had died in pain. But his face was swollen, darkened, and absolutely expressionless.

She knew that they would inevitably have married. Both families had expected it. The funeral time was not hard. It was like something happening in a movie. She wished only that they could have created a new life within her that last time there in the cleft in the hillside, so that in some way there would be preserved that thin tanned face and the look of him so that he would not be so completely dead. It had been clear to her that she would have to get away from that place where he always stood, waiting for her, just out of sight around every corner. The wish to go to school in Johnston seemed a good enough answer. It was also clear that there would never be anyone else. Never.

She was related to Gus's dead wife. He missed his wife badly. Something about her seemed to remind Gus of the way his wife had been when they had both been young. In an odd way it seemed to help him to have her around. One night, a year and a half ago, they had been alone in the house. The others were out. She had decided to go to bed early. She came out of the bathroom to go to her room and found Gus standing in the hall. He looked at her very oddly. She had to go by him to get to her room. He caught her and put his strong arms around her and breathed quickly against her hair. She stood very still and cold for a time, and then sensed his loneliness and his need. And she sensed also a physical stirring within herself that seemed aside and apart from what she had felt in her mind for Peter. She gave herself to him in her room. In the act she found a release she had not expected. Afterward he cried and spoke to her in her parents' tongue, which she could understand but not speak well, calling himself an evil man. In the darkness she told him of Peter, and made him understand. She said they had both lost the most important one. She said she would marry him, if he would be willing to do that.

They were married two weeks later, to the consternation of the family, to the heavy sour amusement of Anna. And the marriage, for Jana, turned out to be something entirely unanticipated. Gus forgot his grief in the joys of the young body of his bride. He grew visibly younger. He was a good virile strength to be with in the night, a good one to laugh with in the daytime. He made her small gifts of tenderness, and her heart grew warm toward him.

With the news of Henry's death, he changed utterly. Within days he lost all the youth she had brought to him. He was no longer a lover. He was a sag-shouldered old man who slept beside her. She had touched him timidly a few times, with the courage of her need, only to have him mutter something incomprehensible and turn heavily away from her. She tried dozens of little ways to reawaken his desire for her, not only because she had learned to need him, but also because she thought that it would help him, that it would give him some little moments of forgetfulness. In the end she began to realize that to him she was now daughter rather than wife. And she resigned herself to tension and to nervousness, hoping that they would soon fade, hoping that the body would slowly readjust itself.

Tonight he had told her of Teena, and he had held her close in the big bed, his slow tears dropping hot against her shoulder. Being held close had finally begun to stir her, in spite of her wish merely to hold him and comfort him. She had restrained herself for as long as she could and then expressed her need in a way that was unmistakable to him, only to have him fling himself away from her and roll over, huddled in a grief he no longer wished to share. After a long time he had fallen asleep, and she lay in the darkness and tried to think of dull and trivial things.

At seven o'clock Tuesday evening, during the long June twilight, the store was closing. Walter locked the door as the last customer, a small boy with a loaf of bread, left and went behind the counter to help Bonny cash up. Rick was rearranging the meat case, taking some of the items into the cooler. Dover, the new boy, was filling the trash cans in the back behind the storeroom and lugging them around one by one to the curb out front for early-morning collection. Gus was working on the vegetables in the display case, snipping off wilted leaves with his thumbnail, picking out the spoiled tomatoes and tossing them into a small broken hamper that Dover would place out front. Jana had swept out and she stood in the left side of the display window taping to the inside of the windows the signs Walter had lettered indicating specials for tomorrow. The truck had driven in from the last delivery and Vern Lockter was tossing a few empty cartons into the storeroom. Everyone worked doggedly and silently. In past years the time of closing had been a good part of the day. Jokes and a few cans of beer opened and talk about the day's business. But on this Tuesday night there was no talk. Just the low murmur of Walter and Bonny, checking the tape and machine totals, the wet splash of spoiled tomatoes, the click-chunk of the cooler door, the faint acid buzzing of the neon.

Jana stepped down out of the window and straightened the display she had moved aside. The day was done. The long evening was ahead of her, a long tunnel with a promise of restless sleep at the far end of it.

At seven-thirty they were finished and they left the store, leaving the night light on. The big table was set in the kitchen. With Dover taking Teena's place, there was the same number as before, seven. Gus and Jana, Walter and Doris, Vern, Rick, and Jimmy. Anna never ate with them. She ate after the others had finished, and while they ate she would plod from stove to table, clinking the cupboard dishes, serving slowly, expressionlessly. The food was plain and heavy. Jana looked along the table. Vern had just come downstairs. He did not eat with them as consistently as Rick Stussen, and when he did eat with them he was usually late coming to the table, as he spent quite a bit of time dressing for the evening. Tonight he was still in work clothes, though he had changed to a fresh T shirt.

Doris said, acid-sweet, "What happened to the fashion plate? Losing your touch, Vern?"

"Going to rearrange some stock to make more room to make up the orders. How about coming out after, and seeing what you think of the idea?"

"Sure," Jana said.

Gus had eaten with his usual galloping haste. He stood up, still chewing, dropped his balled napkin on his plate, mumbled something almost inaudible, and left the kitchen to go to the living room and spend his usual three hours staring blindly at the television screen.

Doris said, "What makes *him* so gay tonight?"

"Lay off, will you?" Walter said.

"Oh, certainly. Lay off. The precious little darling of his had to go take a cure, and who around here gives a damn about how I feel? Does anybody ever worry about me? You'd never know around here I was going to give him a grandchild."

Walter put his fork down and said evenly, "Shut up."

"You don't give a damn, do you?" She banged her coffee cup down. "You know what I want from you, Mr. Nasty? I want you to take me to a movie, much as it hurts you. And I want you wearing a necktie and a coat. I'm not going with you again with you looking like a slob."

Walter sighed and picked up his fork. "O.K., O.K. A movie. Anything."

"The show at the Central looks good," Bonny said. They all looked at her. They had learned to accept her silences, and it was a faint shock to have her volunteer information.

Walter said tentatively, "You want to come, maybe?"

"If you don't mind, either of you."

"That would be swell, Bonny," Doris said, with more warmth than the situation called for, and then immediately blushed. Stussen walked in to sit and look at the television.

"Maybe Jimmy would like to come along too?" Bonny said.

The boy blushed. "Sure. I'd like to."

Vern finished his pie, lit a cigarette, and said, "Want to go to work now, Jana?"

"Sure."

She walked ahead of him down the steps from the kitchen, and along the narow shed pasageway to the one door of the store that was left unlocked because it could be reached only through the kitchen. The market was dark except for the red neon ring around the wall clock. The long self-service counters were shadowy.

They went into the storeroom. Vern kicked a box out of the way and turned on the single bulb. The light was harsh.

He said, "See how it's cramped in here? Now those cases of number-ten cans of juice don't move fast. And they aren't stacked high enough. I figure if we stack them high along that wall, it'll give us more room to work in, and I won't have such a hell of a job sorting the orders and loading them right. What do you think?"

"I guess it's all right, Vern."

"O.K. I'll do it. Stick around and see what you think."

"Let me help."

"You don't have to, Jana."

"I don't mind lifting."

She helped him stack the cases. She could not reach the highest row, so she stood aside and watched him swing them easily up and shove them in place. They sorted by brand, so there would be no need to pull out a case in the middle of one of the stacks. She leaned against the wall by the light and watched the play of his back muscles under the T shirt, watched the cording of his arms. She felt as though, in spite of the length of time he had lived there, she had never known him. There was a funny remoteness about him. Sort of like Bonny, and yet not remote in the same way. But Bonny was acting different lately.

"There!" he said, dusting his hands together.

"It makes a lot more room." Near the corner was a long low row of other cases. She said, "How about those?"

"They can stay as they are for now, hey?"

He turned off the light and she turned toward the doorway and ran into his arm. For a moment she didn't realize that what he had done was brace his right hand against the wall. It confused her to be blocked in that way.

"What are you doing?" she asked, speaking low because of the darkness. She tried to duck under his arm, but he lowered it. She turned the other way and found she was trapped there, between his arms. It scared her that he didn't speak.

She knocked his right arm out of the way and plunged toward the dark doorway. Just as she reached the doorway, his hands came around her from behind, pulling her back against him, holding her there. She knew she should fight him, should struggle and call out. But his hands on her started a trembling that seemed to come up from her knees, a weak trembling that held her there, head bowed, pulled back hard against him as he dropped his lips to the side of her neck, nuzzling her neck, breathing into her hair. He pulled her slowly back into the dark storeroom, moving her, turning her slowly. The edge of the low stack of cartons cut the backs of her calves and she went down slowly, taking great shuddering breaths, feeling as if, under her warm skin, all her flesh and bone and muscle had turned to a warm help-less fluid. He was harsh with her, and it was over quickly.

She lay in darkness and heard him move about the room. Her breathing was beginning to slow when the harsh light came on, shocking her into a dazed scram-bling. She sat up. He stood by the light switch tapping a cigarette out of the pack. The overhead light gave him a black and white look, like a sharp photograph.

"Stop your damn sniffling," he said quietly. And she realized that was the first he had spoken since turning off the light. It made the tears come faster, but she tried to stop the crying sound. He was looking at her as if he hated her. It was as if he had punished her, had wanted to hurt her.

"You . . . shouldn't have."

"Me? *I* shouldn't have? Honey, you don't want to start putting the blame off on me. It seemed to me like it was both of us, Jana."

"If Gus ever finds out, he'll—"

"I imagine he could be a rough old guy about some-thing like this. Figuring on telling him?"

"No. Oh, no!" She felt dulled and sated. He seemed to be standing a long way off, at the far end of some enormous echoing room. It seemed to take vast effort to stand up. She smoothed the crumpled skirt with the palms of her hands, combed at her ruffled hair with her fingers. He tapped ashes from his cigarette on the store-room floor.

"We can arrange this better next time," he said.

"No. I don't want to do it again, Vern."

"You did once. What difference does it make now? One time or forty times. It adds up to the same thing, doesn't it? You liked it. So we'll arrange it better next time. I've got it figured out. I know the mornings the old guy leaves at four to go to the farmers' market. He went this morning. He goes Thursday. He goes on Satur-day. I'll see you about four-thirty Thursday."

"Not there. Not in our room."

"Keep your voice down, damn it. You can't come up on the third floor. I know how to walk like a cat, honey. How can we miss?"

"I won't do it!"

"You will, Jana, because if you don't, I'm going to do a little heavy-handed hinting about your rubbing up against me, and I don't know how long I can hold out. And I won't hint to the old man. I'll hint to Doris and let her carry the ball."

He dropped the cigarette and put his heel on it.

"You wouldn't do that."

"Yes, I would."

"But you act like you . . . hate me or something. Why do you want to do that?"

"Why shouldn't I want to come see you Thursday morning? My God, I'm normal. And you're a very pleasant bundle, honey."

She walked by him, not speaking. She heard him click off the storeroom light and follow her. He caught up with her, casually, in the shed passageway, put his arm around her, pinched the flesh of her waist hard between his fingers and the heel of his hand.

"Thursday, then?"

She made a faint sound of agreement. She felt shamed as though she could never look anyone squarely in the eyes again. Anna was sitting alone at the big table, eating. She gave them a stolid glance and shoveled another forkful between the slow-moving jaws.

Jana went in and sat in the living room. Three girls in shorts were tap-dancing in unison on the TV screen. Jana looked at Gus's stone face. His hands, half curled, rested on his massive thighs. She watched for a time and then made herself go over and kiss Gus lightly on the lips before going up to bed. She took a bath as hot as she could bear it, lowering herself inch by inch into the steaming water, toweling herself harshly afterward until her skin tingled and glowed.

She went to bed, yawning in the darkness, lying loose-bodied in the darkness, trying not to think about it and trying not to think about Thursday morning when she would be alone in darkness, as she was now, and the door would open with stealth and she would hear him softly crossing the room toward her marriage bed. Yet just thinking about that spiraled an expectant excitement within her. And the expectancy heightened her sense of guilt and sense of shame, because she knew that she would welcome him. As he said, it was done. And if it were done again, it would make no difference. It had happened, and after all, it was Gus's fault. What did he expect? For her to stop being a woman because he stopped being a man? It was his fault. All his fault. And Vern didn't hate her. He had only acted that way because he was odd and shy and perhaps frightened. And he would never hint to Doris. That had just been a threat. When you looked at it squarely, it was Gus's fault. They would be very careful. Nothing would happen. They would not be caught. Gus did not want her. Vern did. It would be all right. And she was not to blame, not for any of it.

She fought the guilt, feeling that she chased it back into a remote corner of her mind. It hid there, out of sight.

She felt the sleep coming. She felt it roll up against her, deep and black. A sleep like none she had felt in months. She felt as though, with each exhalation, she sank a bit deeper into the warm bed. There was no tension in her. She floated down and down into the soothing blackness.

Chapter Fifteen

At eleven o'clock on Wednesday morning Paul Darmond looked up from the papers on his desk as
Lieutenant Rowell came into his small office in the courthouse, walking with his bandy-legged strut. Rowell
shoved a chair closer to the wall, sat in it, and tilted it
back against the wall.

"How's the soul-saving going, Preach?"

"Business as usual."

"You sure get yourself around. I've been fighting the
U.S. government. They tried to tell me they'd handle
this one. I told them it was in my back yard, and anything going on in my back yard is my business."

"You got those three kids?"

"On Monday. The Delaney girl. Fitzgerald. Derrain.
One other boy and two more girls. And two pushers
working the high school. A very pretty picture. Delaney,
Fitzgerald, and Derrain had set up a deal in a crumb-
bum hotel, with the Delaney girl turned pro for junk
money, setting up the other two girls on the same pitch,
and with the Fitzgerald boy and the Derrain boy front-
ing for them."

"What was the home situation with the three names
I gave you?"

Rowell shrugged. "The Delaney girl's old lady is a
dipso. The Fitzgerald kid's people both work a night
shift, sleep all day, live in a crummy apartment. Derrain's
people got dough and no sense. The woman isn't his
mother. There was a divorce in the picture. You know
how it goes. All three families. The same yak. Not my
baby. Not my sweet Ginny. Not my darling, my Bucky.
There must be some mistake, Officer. My baby would
never do such terrible things. I get it through their heads
finally that there's no mistake. Then they want a break
for their precious babies. Take it easy on them, Officer.

They didn't realize what they were doing. It always follows the same pattern. So I have to make it clear I'm booking them for everything I can. That's my job. It's up to the judge, once they've had a cure at the county hospital, to be lenient if he wants to. I tossed that Fitz in a cell and broke him in four hours. He and Derrain mugged three guys in the last month, operating from Derrain's car, with the Delaney girl acting as lookout. I talked to the school nurse. There's some other little nests of users in the school. We'll clean up what we can. You sneaked that Varaki girl out from under, Preach. I want to rattle a little information out of her, too."

"She won't be back for a while."

"I can wait."

"Let it lay, Andy. Once she's straightened out I'll get everything she knows and tell you if there's any additional information worth working on."

"We can talk about that later, Preach. I came in to talk about the Dover kid. It looks like that's no place for him, wouldn't you say?"

"Why the sudden concern?"

"I don't like you putting a mess of bad eggs in one of my baskets. A tramp and two one-time losers and a junkie in one household. I don't like it. It means trouble. I don't like that Lockter. He's too smooth. He's working some kind of an angle. I can smell it. If he's working an angle, Preach, putting that new kid in there is just giving him an assistant so he can work the angle a little better, whatever it is."

"If you're right, Dover wouldn't go in with him."

"God, you make me tired sometimes. A wrongo is a wrongo, no matter how you—"

"Not half as tired as you make me, Andy. Go ahead. Lean on Mr. Lockter. Out of the group I've got right now, I'd say he's the poorest risk. I've never got to him."

"My God, that's something for *you* to say."

"And I'd say the Dover boy is one of the best risks. He's going to come out all right."

"Unless he sees a chance too good to miss, you mean."

"Someday, Andy, something is going to happen that'll put you on my side of the fence."

"Reform your kids, Preach. Don't try to work on me. I've got enough troubles. Just make some other arrangements for Dover, will you?"

"Let's let it ride, Andy."

Rowell sighed, made a grotesque gesture of despair, and left.

Paul turned his attention back to his work, but he could not concentrate. It was as though Bonny stood close behind him, almost touching him, and he had only to turn the scarred and creaking swivel chair to be able to look up into the gray of her eyes and fold the slimness of her waist in his arms, the fresh clean fragrance of her in his nostrils.

He could isolate, pin down the exact moment when it had happened, there on the sun-spotted terrace with the brook sounds, with the look of her across from him, her head tilted a bit as she listened to something he was saying. She had listened with head tilted and then her gray eyes widened with a warm amusement, and her chin came up a bit and her round throat had been full of soft laughter, and in her amusement her glance had moved across his eyes, faltered, returned, focused then with a small narrowing look, almost of alarm, as her laughter faded. In that moment she had ceased to be the widow of Henry Varaki, ceased to be a person he could help in any way, and became to him a desirable woman, something of lilt and fragrance and need.

He remembered how he had talked to her, remembered his own ponderous, stuffy conversation. He thought of what she must think of him and he could not help flushing.

He got up from his desk and took the single stride to the dusty window and looked down at the June street below, at the paper-littered green of the courthouse lawn.

Betty had said once, "Paul, you have a knack of suffering about everything. You spend half your time thinking of what you should have done or should not have done, long after it's finished and over and quite through."

Now, Betty, you who understood me so well, you could explain to me why this is happening. It was never to happen again. You were enough for a lifetime. I want her. I want her so badly that now I think of how she stood there, throwing words at me the way a child would throw stones, telling me I could take her there by the gray stones. She has been badly hurt, by herself. Yet she has a great pride. She won't accept pity. If she interprets my interest as charity, she will despise me. I know she has been used by many men. When I think of that, something turns over slowly inside me, like the first warning of nausea. Yet intellectually I can tell myself that it was not Bonny who was used. The men used her body, and her body was the device by which she was punishing herself for original sin. Somehow, some way, I must be able to tell her that it's not pity, it's not charity, it's not lust. Nor is it the romantic love of adolescence. It's a woman I want. I want her, mind, soul, body. Which is something you must understand, because it's the way I wanted you. This is not lesser, or greater. It's the same thing. I was not made to be alone.

In this year I have felt myself edging toward a funereal dryness, a crotchety exactitude. Now it's time to come alive again, Betty.

He knew, standing there, that if he followed his impulse blindly it would take him to her to stand with blundering adoration in front of her, content to look upon her face. He half shrugged and smiled at himself and went back to his desk.

He phoned Dr. Foltz and asked about Teena.

"She's a very disturbed child, Paul. The usual malnutrition. We're giving her glucose until she can keep food on her stomach. We're watching her carefully."

"What's the emotional response?"

"The usual thing. Sullen, bitter, rebellious, unresponsive. I got the lab reports on her yesterday. Outside of the addiction and being run down physically, she's all right."

"She was a very happy kid, Doctor."

"She's going to be a very unhappy kid for quite a while, particularly when the usual remorse sets in. Somebody will have to keep an eye on her pretty closely after she's released."

"I have somebody lined up, I think."

"Good. I hate to see them slip back into addiction. If the first cure doesn't take, it's a fair gamble that no subsequent one will, either."

"Let me know when she'll be ready for the first visitor, will you, please?"

"Of course, Paul."

Paul sat for a time with his hand resting on the dead phone in its cradle, and then he got up and went to lunch alone.

Chapter Sixteen

IT WAS on Wednesday that Bonny knew she was becoming aware of those around her on some other basis than their relationship to her. She had spent long hours since the lunch with Paul Darmond, going over and over what he had said to her, trying in every way to discount the sharpness of the scalpel.

Preoccupation with self had been a comforting insulation. You could hide within self, and look out of a narrow place at the world, the way an animal might crouch and be aware only of those who passed by and showed any interest in the cave's darkness.

Paul had roughly stripped away the insulation and left the nerve ends shrill. She needed the warmth and comfort of the cave, but he had made it impossible for her to return.

It was like learning to live again. Years had been spent in the dim cave. Now she had come out of the dark place, had, rather, been hauled out physically, and stood naked in a bright place peopled with those she had been aware of only one-dimensionally.

On Wednesday morning in the bath she stood with her foot on the edge of the tub, drying neatly between her toes, and she stopped and looked at the slim ivory of her foot, examining herself in new awareness. This was the body that, in all justice, should have recorded faithfully the crumbled years. Yet the body had no look of violent use, and there was neither justice nor fairness in that. The firm, almost virginal look of her was like a taunt. Like a gift given in contempt. Thus, in giving it again, it would be something she had neither saved nor nurtured. And thus a gift of little value to the giver. She had seen the familiar shifting unrest in his eyes, and she felt again the warmth of his hand as it cupped her face. She slipped into her robe and belted it closely around the body that suddenly felt flushed and aware of him.

Jana was alone at the big table in the kitchen when she arrived. Anna nodded to her and expressionlessly cracked two more eggs into the frying pan.

"Good morning," Bonny said. "It's a lovely day."

Jana seemed to become only gradually aware that she was no longer alone. She looked blankly at Bonny and at last smiled, almost shyly. She seemed to come back from a far place that was not pleasant to her.

"Is anything wrong?" Bonny asked.

Jana, surprisingly flushed. "No, there isn't anything wrong," she said too insistently. "Nothing at all."

Anna set the juice glass and the breakfast plate down in front of Bonny. She set them down heavily. Jimmy Dover came quickly in and said, "I guess I'm sort of late."

"Walter won't open up for another ten minutes," Bonny told him. She turned to Jana. "Are we the last?"

Jana blushed again. "Vern and Doris aren't down yet."

Her statement puzzled Bonny. There was no point in mentioning Doris. She never got up before ten. As she ate she examined Jana more carefully. Even in her preoccupation with herself, she had been remotely aware that Jana had acted restless and discontented for the last few months, while the old man had been lost in the cold remoteness of his grief for his son. Now the constant blushings gave Jana a look of rosiness, almost of soft contentment.

Vern came down with his automatic smile and his look of composure. And Bonny saw Jana blush again and conspicuously avoid looking at Vern. Bonny, with her new clarity and awareness, covertly studied Vern. A very cold and very handsome young man. And with, about him, a faint warning note of danger. A sleek young man, and a young woman of a husky ripeness, and an old man whom death had turned vague.

It was a situation so trite that it seemed almost implausible to her.

It's none of my business, she told herself. Their dangerous little game is nothing that concerns me. Yet even as she told herself she should not be concerned, she seemed to feel the presence of Paul Darmond close behind her, see even a mocking accusation in his eyes. No

man is an island unto himself. She could tell herself that
in return for their taking her in, she had given them work.
Service in return for warmth. Yet in return for warmth,
perhaps warmth itself is the only acceptable currency.

She watched Jana get up and go around the table,
taking her plate over to the counter. Bonny saw Jana
turn and hesitate and then take the big coffee pot from
the stove and carry it over and fill Vern's cup. She saw
the flick of Vern's eyes up at her pink face. Vern was
alone on the far side of the table. She saw his shoulder
move a bit and saw the shudder that went through Jana.
Saw the shudder and the stillness and the eyes go half
closed as the black stream of the coffee slid beyond the
cup rim to splash in the saucer. Jana took the pot back to
the stove and Vern looked coolly across at Bonny, meeting her glance, raising one eyebrow in an expression both
quizzical and triumphant.

It was a male look that she had seen many times before.
And she knew, seeing it, that she would talk to Jana
—that the talk would be awkward, perhaps vicious, most
probably ineffectual, but talk she would. For a thing
like this could end in that ultimate violence. And this
house had seen enough of violence.

She knew that there would be no chance until evening.
She took over the cash register as the store opened, taking
the currency and change from the brown canvas sack and
counting it into the drawer. Gus Varaki did the day's
tasks like a sleepwalker. Rick Stussen cut meat deftly,
thin blade flashing as he sharpened it, cleaver chunking
the block, scraps plopping wetly into the box by the
block. Walter worked in a morose silence. During mid-
morning Doris paid one of her rare visits to the store
to get a pack of cigarettes. Her manner was that of a
princess forced to visit the kitchens to complain about
the service. Bonny was startled by the look Walter gave
her. Walter looked at his wife with a fury that made his
mouth tremble.

Bonny began to watch him more closely. It was odd
to come out of a selfish trance and see, so clearly, the
forces of violence surrounding her. Teena first, and now
Jana, and soon, perhaps, Walter.

One of the wholesale houses made the usual cash delivery at two o'clock. The delivery man was stooped and
gaunt, with a collapsed-looking mouth.

"Can you give me my thirty-two bucks, Red? Or we gotta whistle for Walter?"

Walter came from across the store. He took the bill and studied it, went behind the cash register, and rang up $32.12 paid out and morosely counted out the money. "You eaten yet, Bonny?"

"I haven't had a chance yet."

"I'll get Jana off those phone orders. Go on in and eat."

Bonny was back on the job at two-thirty. During a lull at three o'clock she checked her totals, found an additional fifty dollars run up as paid out. That checked roughly with the dwindled size of the cash stacks. She thought no more about it until a customer paid with a rare two-dollar bill. As she did not want to leave it in the regular cash section of the drawer, where it might be paid out in error as a five or a ten, she put it in the compartment with the receipted bills. Something about that compartment left her with a distant creeping of suspicion. As soon as she has a chance she looked again. There was no longer a receipted bill for $32.12. There was a receipted bill for $82.12. The penciled three had been turned deftly into an eight, and a five written in front of an item of less than ten dollars. The alteration would stand a casual glance, but when she looked at it closely she could see the alteration had been made with a softer pencil than the one used to make out the original bill. She stared at it closely and then turned, with the altered receipted bill in her hand, and looked across the store. Walter was standing beyond one of the racks, looking directly at her, standing without movement and looking into her eyes. There was a stub of red pencil in his teeth. She put the bill back in the compartment and made herself turn away slowly, casually. The register would balance. The fifty paid out would match the amount the bill had been increased.

It gave her an instantaneous re-evaluation of Walter Varaki. She had thought of him as a wife-soured man, working dutifully at a job he did not care for, in order to help his father. A meek, submissive, hag-ridden man whose life was colorless.

it must have been he who had stolen. It could not een anyone else. Certainly not Jana. And not Gus, from himself. Rick Stussen never touched the cash register. It could, of course, have been the new boy, but that was improbable. He would not have been in the store alone. He would not, as yet, know the routines well enough. Vern was still out on delivery.

It had to be Walter, and this could not be the first time.

She saw the ramifications of the act. Discovery of shortages would point invariably at her, at Vern, and at Jimmy Dover. Of the three of them, she was the logical choice. It frightened her. There was one person to turn to, and quickly. Paul Darmond would know what she should do, and yet . . . She began to think of the old man. One son dead. One son a thief. His daughter a drug addict. His wife faithless. Could a man stand that? And she realized anew that she was thinking now of someone else, thinking of the effect of circumstance upon another, rather than upon herself. And it gave her a strange warm pride to think she was now capable of this—a pride in herself and a feeling of gratitude to Paul Darmond.

The day ended and the store closed and the meal was eaten by all the people with their closed faces and their inward-looking eyes. An old house, and a high-ceilinged kitchen, and in the air a stale smell of regret and fear and lust.

She caught Jana on the stairs. "Could you come on up to my room for a minute?"

Jana looked at her curiously. "What do you want? I got to change my shoes. These are hurting me."

"There's something I want to ask you, in private."

"Sure. I'll come on up in a minute."

Bonny went up to her room, took off her slacks and hung them up, and changed to a wool skirt. She decided against putting a record on. She sat on the edge of the bed and turned the pages of a magazine. Jana tapped on the door and came in and closed it behind her. She went over to the bedside chair and sat, her feet in wide broken slippers.

"What did you want to ask me about?"

Bonny had thought of the dozens of ways she could say it. But none of them seemed any good.

"The cigarettes are beside you there."

"Thanks, not right now."

"Jana, are you . . ."

"Am I what? What's the matter with you, anyway?"

"Are you sleeping with Vern Lockter?"

The question made a great stillness in the air of the small room. Jana's eyes went wide and she put one hand to her throat. Then she turned and reached for the cigarettes, jiggled one out of the package, and lit it tremblingly.

"What gave you that kind of a crazy idea?"

"The way you looked at each other at breakfast. The way you kept blushing. The way he touched you when he thought nobody could see him. The way you spilled the coffee. The way you look. The way you're acting right now. You can't kid me, Jana. I know too damn much about it and you know too damn little. If you knew anything, Lockter is the last one you'd pick."

Jana's eyes turned bright and angry. "What is it to you?"

"I live here. I'm Gus's daughter-in-law."

"It isn't anything to you. It isn't anything at all to you. What do you think it's like, an old man like that, beside you and never touching you, worn out, no good? What do you think it's like? My God!"

Bonny leaned forward. "You're being a damn fool."

"I don't care. I don't care. He's young and I love the way he walks and looks . . . so strong and slim."

"He's a poisonous type, Jana. And it's dangerous. Right here, under your husband's roof, with a man he took in when that man was in trouble."

"It's my business what I do."

"It's mine too."

"I can't see that. You're sticking your nose in where it isn't wanted. What do you know about it?"

"Right from wrong. And so do you."

"A hell of a lot you know about right and wrong. We all know about you. Who are you to tell me what I ought to do? I like your damn nerve. Maybe you want him for yourself."

"I wouldn't touch that particular young man with eleven-foot poles, Jana."

"Maybe you think you're too good for him."

"Maybe I do."

"A tramp like you! Who's kidding who?"

Bonny looked down at her own fisted hand, resting on the wool of the skirt. She did not speak. She heard Jana make a choked sound and she looked over and saw that

Jana had bent forward from the waist, forehead against her close-pressed knees, rolling her head helplessly from side to side. Bonny went over and knelt beside the chair and put her arm across Jana's shoulders.

Jana said, "I didn't mean to say that."

"It's all right. That isn't the important thing right now. The important thing is this business with Vern. Has it been going on long?"

"No."

"How long?"

"Just . . . since yesterday. After supper. Out in the storeroom. Just that once."

"His idea?"

"I can't look at you and tell you. He just . . . took hold of me. I didn't know he was going to. And I . . . couldn't fight or anything. I wanted him to, as soon as he grabbed me. I know it's terrible, but I can't do anything. Any time he wants to do it again, it will be the same way. I can't stop thinking about him. It's like by doing it that way, he sort of owns me. Do you know what I mean?"

"Yes, my dear. I know what you mean."

Jana lifted her stained face. "I can't stop him. So I got to make out like it's all right, haven't I? It happened once. What difference does it make if it keeps on happening?"

"Did he say that?"

"Yes. He said that to me, afterward."

"You mustn't let it happen again."

"I know I shouldn't. But I *want* it to happen again. He . . . isn't kind. It's like he hates me. But even that's better than nothing."

"Do you want help?"

"I guess I do, Bonny."

"We've got to get him away from here, Jana. I think I know how it can be done. I think I know who can handle it."

"I . . . don't want him to go away."

"But you know that's best, don't you?"

"I guess so."

"If your husband found out, Jana, something very terrible might happen."

"He'd kill both of us."

"And Vern can certainly understand that. He knows Gus well enough to understand that. I can't understand why Vern is willing to take such a crazy chance. He isn't a hot-blooded type. This is part of some plan, Jana. See if you can be strong enough not to let him have you again if he tries before I can . . . make arrangements."

"I'll try, but—"

"I know. I know how sometimes you're . . . vulnerable. Does Paul Darmond live far from here?"

"Are you going to tell him?"

"Don't be worried."

"I didn't want anybody to know. It makes me feel so ashamed."

"When it's right, Jana, you never feel ashamed. You want the world to know. The things you want to hide are always bad."

"I guess I can't stop you."

"No. You can't."

"You act so different, Bonny. So . . . different."

"I feel different. That's a long story. I'll tell you someday."

Jana told her how to find Paul's apartment. It was only six blocks away. She walked Jana slowly to the door of the room and, on impulse, kissed her cheek quickly.

"Feel better, Jana?"

"I don't know yet."

"Try not to go near him. That will make it easier."

Jana didn't answer. She hurried toward the stairs, her shoulders a bit hunched, her head down, moving heavily, as though a lot of the warm life had gone out of the sturdy peasant body.

Chapter Seventeen

IT WAS nearly nine o'clock as Bonny walked through the dark street to Paul Darmond's apartment. She was glad she was able to walk away from the neoned sections. Here the sidewalks were narrow, the slabs tilted by the elm roots, the footing in the dark places uncertain. She walked through a neighborhood of two-family houses, catching glimpses through the lighted windows of feet up, newspapers spread wide, kids doing homework at the cleared dining-room tables.

Two more blocks to go. Ahead she saw the white glare of a corner drugstore, the answering brightness of a gas station. She passed the bright area and as she moved into darkness again, a car cruised beside her. The beam of the spotlight pinned her as she walked, so that she seemed to walk on in one spot, as though on a treadmill.

"I thought I said something about staying off my streets, Bonny," Rowell said, with that mocking friendliness more deadly than rage.

She walked on for two steps and stopped and turned to face the car, hand shielding her eyes from the glare. The car was stopped. The light was changed a bit to shine against her body, leaving her face in relative darkness.

"Come here, Bonny."

She hesitated. She felt cold and careful, as though she were being forced to walk across a narrow steel beam forty stories above the street. She walked toward the round glowing eye of the spot and stopped three feet from it, able to make out the dark glints of the car body, a vague face to the right of the spotlight.

"Have you been knocking off a few drinks, kid?"

"No."

"Out looking for a little fun, maybe?"

"No."

"Maybe you're out looking for a little business."

"I don't know what you mean."

"Bonny, you're quite a kid. What's the new act?"

"I don't know what you mean."

"The lady act. Where'd you pick that up?"

It was an effort to keep from saying the words he was trying to goad her into. "I was on my way to see Paul Darmond, Lieutenant."

"Now, isn't that cute? Seeing the Preach, hey? Hand me your purse, honey."

"Why?"

"Give it to me quick. I want to keep this friendly, don't you?"

She handed her purse toward the half-seen face. It was snatched roughly out of her hand. She saw it vaguely under the dash lights, heard the click of the fastener. After a moment the fastener clicked again. The car door opened.

"Come here."

She knew he had turned sideways in the car seat. She took another rigid step, stopped when his knee touched her. She stood, instinctively closing her eyes. His hard hands patted her quickly, efficiently, from throat to knees.

"They ever take a knife off you on the Coast?"

"Why don't you ask them?"

"I'm asking you, baby."

"No."

The purse was thrust against her and she took it and took a quick step back away from him.

"Did I tell you you could leave?"

"No."

"Come here."

She moved forward again. She listened for ten long seconds to the muted sound of the motor, the faint rasp of his breathing.

"Now you can take off, kid."

She did not trust herself to say anything. She turned and walked on legs that had turned wobbly and uncertain. She walked and she said softly, "Aaaaaah, God! God!" Her teeth chattered and she shut her jaw hard, achingly hard. She remembered what Paul had warned her about. She stopped under a street light and opened her purse with cold awkward fingers. Nothing had been added or removed.

She had walked the high narrow beam and had managed not to look down at the beetle cars and the slow ants that were people. It meant, somehow, that next time she could stand a beam that was a bit narrower, a bit longer.

Here the heavy houses grew close to the sidewalk and she knew it was his block, but it was too dark to see the numbers. She saw an old-fashioned bay window with yellowed lace curtains and saw him standing in the room in shirt sleeves, unknotted necktie dangling. She went up the steps quickly and the front door was unlocked and his had to be the first door on the left. She rapped, a nervous staccato, and he opened the door, the light behind him.

"Bonny!"

"Paul, I . . . I . . ." And her teeth started chattering again. He pulled her gently into the room and closed the door by reaching over her shoulder to push against it, and turned that gesture into an enfolding one, holding her against his chest. She felt the hard angle of his jaw against her temple, and she stood against him, her locked fists under her chin, trembling.

He held her and the shaking slowly went away. At last she looked up at him and managed to smile and made a small face and he released her. "I'm sorry," she said.

"What happened?"

"Rowell stopped me, just down the street."

"Why on earth did you walk over here? You should have phoned, or taken a cab or something."

"I didn't want any of them to know I was coming over. I left sort of quietly."

"For Rowell to . . . Damn it, Bonny, it just isn't fair."

"It's a way of paying, I guess."

"What's the matter with me? Sit down. Do you want a drink?"

"No, thanks, Paul." She sat on the couch and looked at the room for the first time. It was a characterless, transient place. His books were there, and a picture, and that was all.

The picture was a studio portrait of a girl with something very alive in her face.

"Is that your wife, Paul?"

He glanced over at the picture. "She never liked that picture of her. I guess she never liked any picture of herself. She hated to have them taken. I had to bully her to get that one."

"She was very lovely."

She dug her cigarettes out of her purse, and he came over and held a light for her. "Why did you come to see me?"

"The other day you . . . taught me something. It took a while for it to take effect, I guess. It's hard to take a long look at yourself and understand that what motivates you is self-pity and guilt. I've been . . . more outgoing since then. Terrible expression. I mean it's been like waking up and looking around and seeing where you are. You see things you didn't see when you were being a zombie."

He sat on a straight chair, hunched forward, elbows on his knees, smoke rising up through the lean fingers of his right hand.

"And you've seen something you think I should know?" he asked quietly.

"Two things, Paul. I found one out because I've started watching people. I found the other out by accident. They're both bad."

"Is Lockter involved in one?"

"I thought you'd ask that. Yes. Of course. He's seduced Jana."

"Dear Lord!" Paul said. "Is that a hunch?"

"I made her admit it. She's too young for Gus, of course. And lonely and vulnerable, and very earthy. I gather that she didn't exactly put up any struggle. Now she's rebellious and trying to justify herself because, in her heart, she knows that any amount of regret or determination isn't going to do her any good. If he wants her again, it will be just as easy for him as turning on a light. She's the only one who knows I've come to talk to you. She agrees that the best thing would be to get him out of there. I hope you can do it."

"He's no longer on parole. It doesn't give me much leverage."

"Gus has tremendous pride, Paul. And decency. I think he's capable of murderous anger."

"I know he is. It's a very bad situation. I can't somehow see Vern Lockter taking that sort of risk. I thought he was too clever for that." He stood up and paced over to the scarred ornate mantel, tapping a cigarette absently on his thumbnail. "I can think of only one way to handle it. And

I don't think much of the method. Talk to him. I've never had a hell of a lot of success talking to him. He agrees with everything I say, and I get the feeling he's thinking all the time that I'm somebody to humor and ignore. But maybe letting him know that I know what he's up to . . . that might put the fear of God in him."

"Suppose he just denies it?"

"He might do that. If I don't get anywhere, I can see what Andy Rowell can do with him.'

"You wouldn't tell Rowell about it?"

"I wouldn't dare without getting his word first that he'd never use it except to move Lockter along, move him out of the neighborhood."

"You'd take his word?"

"Yes." Paul took a kitchen match off the mantel and struck it on the underside of the mantel and lit his cigarette. "Could that Dover boy take over the deliveries?"

"I think so. He seems very nice, Paul. And intelligent."

"I'll see Lockter tomorrow."

"I told Jana to try to stay away from him. The other thing is very odd, Paul." He listened intently as she told him the story of the altered receipt.

"But if Walter needs money, all he has to do is ask Gus."

"If he needs it for something he can explain, don't you mean?"

"What could he need it for that he couldn't explain? I know how Walter lives, Bonny. He never goes out alone. He couldn't get into gambling trouble or woman trouble because Doris wouldn't give him the chance. Doris keeps an arm lock on him twenty-five hours a day."

"She's insecure, Paul. She's just one of those people who need reassurance so badly that they go around guaranteeing, by the way they act, that they'll never get it. And that makes them nastier. She makes his life hell."

"Which," he said slowly, "is probably the reason for taking the money. When he has enough . . ."

"Of course!" Bonny said. "I can hardly blame the guy. But it will be terrible for Gus. All the luck has gone, Paul. All the luck has gone out of that house. And it's still running away like water, the little bit that's left."

"Even if Gus should find out, he wouldn't go to the law. You know, he realizes somebody has been tapping

the till. He told me. He thought it was Teena. I guess
he didn't make any real effort to check because he was
brooding about Henry."

"What will you do?"

"Tell you to talk to Walter."

"Me! No, Paul."

"Yes, you. You understand Doris better than he does,
I think. Do you think there's any way to handle her? Any
way he could make his life more endurable?"

"I don't know. She'll be vicious and making trouble,
and yet when you show interest in her, she'll suddenly
melt for a few moments. If she weren't so pregnant, I
know what I'd do. I mean, if I were a man. If I were
Walter I'd shake her until her teeth rattled. I'd cuff her
until she was too dazed to cry, and then I'd make love to
her and comfort her, and let her know that the next time
she turned mean, the very same thing would happen. She
doesn't respect him. And I think force is something she
would respect. Walter is too gentle and meek. Almost
frightened of her. It wouldn't astonish me much, Paul, if
treatment like that might turn her into a sweet and ador-
ing wife. There's something very nice under all her wasp-
ishness. But it couldn't be done halfway. That would just
make her worse. But of course, with Doris so pregnant,
it can't be done. She uses that like a weapon, anyway. She
wears her baby like an insult to Walter. And he takes it."

"Talk to Walter, Bonny."

"It may not help."

"What *will* help?"

She thought for a moment, smiled reluctantly. "Nothing else, I guess." She stood up. "I should be getting
back."

"Not the way you came. I'll drive you."

He knotted his tie quickly and put on a jacket. Outside
they got into the car. The motor whispered and caught
and settled into a sputtering roar. He drove down the
alley and out onto the dark street.

He parked by the curb in front of the Varaki house.
There was a light in a second-floor window, and a fainter
one in one of the small windows on the third floor under
the eaves.

She put her hand on the door latch and said, "Thank
you, Paul."

He put his hand on her other wrist and turned off the

car lights. They sat in the darkness. She could not see his face.

"No, Paul," she whispered.

"No what? What are you saying no to?"

"I don't know. Everything, I guess. No to all the things that can't work out. No to whatever you think I am."

He pulled at her, slowly and strongly, and she held herself away from him, and then let out all her breath and came into his arms, feeling a remote surprise at the way, in the cramped little car, they seemed to fit together without awkwardness. His lips were hard and firm against hers, and for a few moments she was conscious of being there in a discouraged little car, kissing a tall stranger, conscious of his worn cuff and slightly frayed collar, a sober and talkative man they called the Preacher. And then her cool watchfulness was melted away in the long kiss, a kiss that somehow destroyed her awareness of him as a lean stranger, and made him forever Paul, a close strength and warmth and need.

Then her face was in the hollow of his throat, and his lips made some inarticulate sound against her hair, and she could hear the slow drum of his heart.

She pushed herself away and her laugh was abrupt and nervous. "You make me feel like a damn girl."

"I know."

"How would you know?"

"For once, Bonny, I don't want to think or explain."

She laughed again, a small quick sound like something breaking. "Let's let explanations wait. Because once we explain it to ourselves, Paul, that's going to be the end of it."

"Is it?"

"Of course." She pressed her palms flat and hard against his cheeks, kissed him lightly on the mouth. He caught her wrists, kissed the palm of each hand, and let her go. She got out of the car and turned and looked in at the darkness where he was for a moment, then slammed the car door hard and went without a word into the house.

She readied herself for bed with great haste, wanting to hold to her mood of glowing excitement. Yet once in darkness she felt it slipping away as inside her the carefully compartmented acid ate through its walls.

What are you, Bonita, to revert to schoolgirl reactions?

What are you pretending to be? A rather pathetic impersonation, my dear. For you can give Paul a rather professional imitation of love, complete with the automatic sighs, the contrived kissings, a tremulousness as fake as a four-dollar violin. Like the imitation of love you gave Henry. Maybe the vividness of the raw memories had become a bit blurred in the past few days because you're coming alive again. But they will not be blurred in Paul's mind. He will always be aware of all the fingerprints on you. He's vulnerable because he's lonely, and you're an attractive wench, and so he's giving emotional overtones to a basic need while you aid and abet.

The spreading acid ate away the dream, and she was taut in her bed. As dawn came inevitably closer, she knew that this was the longest night of her life, longer even than that first night she had spent in jail, in the female tank, in the sick air and the cat sounds.

She heard the sounds in the old house. She heard Jimmy and the old man get up and heard the clatter of the truck as they drove out, leaving the house again in silence. And then she heard a softer sound, a stealthy movement, the creak of a board. She thought what it could be and came quickly out of bed, snatching her dark robe and putting it on. The doorknob was cold in her hand as she turned it slowly. It opened without a sound. She looked toward the head of the stairs, saw the cat creep of movement, saw in the faint light of the stairway window that Vern Lockter was going soft and easy down the stairs. When he was no longer in sight, she went quietly to the stairs. The stair carpet was bristly under her bare feet. She looked cautiously down the darker length of the second-floor hall just in time to see Vern disappear through the door of the bedroom of Gus and Jana. He eased through and she heard a very muted click of the latch on the door. She stood then, waiting for an outcry that she sensed would never come. The old house was silent. There was no flaw in the night stillness. Far off a train made a hooting, a metallic frog in the pond of the night. She shivered then, hearing in the hooting an ancient note of derision. The night was a still violence. She turned and went back up the stairs and down the hallway to her room. She shut the door and threw her robe aside and got into bed and felt a childish need to hide under the bedclothes.

Chapter Eighteen

Vern Lockter drove the Thursday-morning delivery route with ragged impatience. He raced the lights, cut corners, squealed his wheels in the driveways. He thumped the orders on the kitchen tables, trotted back to the truck. He knew that his haste was not making the time go faster, yet he felt as though he had to hurry. It seemed the only way to ease the tension within him. He kept remembering how it had been, the sense of strength and power he had felt when he had walked through the sleeping house.

He remembered how he had stood beside the bed, barely hearing her whisper, "Oh no, oh no, ohno ohno ohno ohno . . ." slurring the words into meaningless incantation. An incantation that had stopped as he had slid in beside her.

And he remembered the half-heard dismal sound of her crying as he had left her.

Doris sat in the dim morning cave of the living room. The life within her kicked lustily and she put the needle into the pincushion and held the palm of her hand against herself and felt the soft thumping against her hand. You could hate it, and hate the thought of the clumsiness and hate the aching back, and remember the awkward and customary discomfort of the moment of conception and hate that too. But then, unaware, would come these moments of a strange warm excitement. Moments, almost, of pride. My son, my daughter, my child.

The joyous moment faded and she snatched up the needle again. What will you have, my child? A thoughtless, meek, stupid, ambitionless father. A stinking inheritance of a weary little market. Oh, God, I wanted so much and now I'm trapped, forever and ever and ever. How did it happen?

Jimmy Dover studied the vegetable rack for a moment. Funny how quick you could start liking something. Pale crisp green of lettuce, dark feathery green of the carrot tops. Royal gleaming eggplant purple. Tomato red.

He liked going out in the truck with the old man in the predawn, when the lights were bright on the stuff that had come in from the farms. They kidded around out there, and they all knew the old man. He kidded too, but in a kind of heavy way, as if he didn't feel like it. He was shrewd, all right, about knowing what to buy, knowing what was best. You could watch him carefully and pick up a lot of tips. And he'd always answer questions. Not like some guys who want to make a dark secret out of anything they know. It was all pretty tricky. There were fifty things to learn about tomatoes alone, and he'd always thought tomatoes were tomatoes, and so what?

There sure was a lot of work to the grocery business, but at the same time there was a lot of fun to it, too. You could see the old man liked it, just from the way he handled stuff. On this night-school pitch it might be a good idea to take courses that would help you in the grocery business. Purchasing methods and calories and bookkeeping and stuff like that. Maybe advertising, too. And that diet stuff. They all seem kind of gloomy around here, though. That Lockter won't give you the time of day. Only time he says anything is when he wants something done right now. Same with that Walter. Rick is a sort of a dumb guy. Bonny is nice, though. And Jana is sort of nice. When the kid gets back, that Teena, maybe she'll cheer them up. They're probably all worried about her. She could be cute once she gets fixed up. It looks like I'm getting through this week O.K. But I wish these people could be more friendly, sort of.

Rick, at the chopping block, with his back to the store, made a quick slit in a T-bone steak that he suspected was going to be tough, fingered the small glossy cylinder out of the pocket of his apron, and thumbed it into the slit. That was the next to the last one of the week. It had become a meaningless game. You do anything enough times and it seems like you stop thinking about it. He wrapped the steak, tied it, snapped off the string, weighed it, and crayoned the price on the outside. He carried it out into the storeroom and gave it to Walter.

He walked solidly back and found two customers waiting. He gave them his big smile and said, "Got some nice pork chops today, ladies."

Teena, in pajamas, canvas slippers, and gray bathrobe, walked down the gravel path slowly with the thin nurse. The sun felt hot. This was the first walk. It felt like coming out of the movies in the middle of the afternoon. Like daylight was surprising. Her legs felt trembly, and the sun hurt her eyes.

"Too fast, honey?" the nurse asked.

"No. This is O.K."

"We can go all the way down to those benches. Then we'll sit a little while and go back."

"O.K."

"Then after we go back you'll finish all your lunch tray today."

"I'm not hungry."

"We got to put some meat on you, honey. You look like a picked chicken."

"I don't care how I look."

"Then after lunch I'll fix you up nice in the solarium where you'll have people to talk to."

"I don't want to talk to anybody."

"Here we are, honey. We can sit in the sun for a little while. Doesn't it feel good, though?"

Gus stood heavily and watched the colorless little man tenderly open his worn case of gleaming brass weights. There were four scales to check in the store. The same little man came in and checked them each time, always with an air of somber dedication. Gus, while watching him, was thinking of Jana, and of her oddness on this morning when he had arisen at four to go with the new boy to the farmers' market. Usually her sleep when he left was that of any healthy young animal. On this morning she had clung to him and asked him not to go. For a time he had tried to be patient with her nonsense, but then in irritation he had pulled his arm from her grasp. Women had strange moods. Jana had always seemed so quiet and patient. And her sweetness of body had brought back, for a time, the energies of younger years. But now there was too much worry. Henry. Teena. Too many cold things to think about.

The Judge sat like a cross child in his hot bath, soaping his body. It had been an unpleasant failure. Guillermo had just used his imagination this time. True, she had been young enough, but filled with a callous, un-co-operative indifference. Damn it, the girl had acted *bored*. That did not flatter a man. And then there was the business of the envelope. A girl of the proper instincts would have accepted it discreetly and tucked it away. But this young person had ripped it open, fanned the three bills, shrugged, and put the bills in her purse. She had made him feel gross and old and ridiculous.

All in all, this was not one of the better weeks. He had the feeling that he had become too fanciful in his handling of the Lockter situation. Perhaps Lockter's talent for melodrama was contagious. Ritchie, whose instincts were usually sound, had listened to the solution and dared to sneer at it. "O.K., Judge, so you're cute. So you maybe got him sewed up right. Me, I would have told him to get in the truck and bring the butcher with him, and someplace along the line I would have a good trustworthy boy in one of Herman's old semi jobs give them the head-on treatment. Like in Fall River last year. Suppose he just turns that butcher into hospital meat?"

"You worry too much, Ritchie."

"You're getting too cute, Judge."

Jana, down on one thick knee putting canned soup on the low rack, grease-penciling the price on the top of each can, glanced guiltily over toward Bonny and saw that some instinct had informed her that Bonny was staring at her. She saw the look in Bonny's eyes and turned hastily back to the task at hand. Bonny knew, somehow. Bonny knew that in spite of her promise, it had happened again. God, she couldn't help it. He was like a knife in her heart. Keen, cold, cruel.

I won't be able to stand it if he goes away. Even if it is a bad thing. Even if it is terrible, the way he does it, like hating, I don't want him to go away.

What had happened to everything?

What is happening to the world?

The driveway that led to the back of the store was on the far side of the big house. Paul parked by the driveway and walked to where he could see the back of the market.

The truck was not there. Lockter would be back soon, probably. He went back to his car and sat behind the wheel to wait. He knew he should be thinking of how he would handle this talk with Lockter, and yet he could not turn his thoughts away from Bonny. She had been so very alive in his arms. And no one could have so perfectly imitated that tremulousness, that nervous laugh. He knew the kiss had moved her. Yet he had the bitter awareness that the next time it would be the same—he would be waiting for some sign of deceit, of pretended passion.

During the wakeful hours of the night he had decided that he wanted to marry her. And he had prayed for the strength to overcome the jealousy that was like rusty iron being pulled through his body. Yet he knew that their salvation in any marriage would be possible only if their physical mating was a strong, good, tender thing. Without that, neither of them would have the strength to stand up under the weight of her past. And so he had decided it necessary for them to be together soon, to find this answer, to go on if the answer could be good, and turn their backs on each other if the answer was wrong.

When the panel delivery truck turned into the drive he got out quickly and waved Vern Lockter to a stop.

"Hi there, Mr. Darmond! What's on your mind?"

"I want to talk to you, Vern."

"O.K. I'll park this wagon and be right back."

Vern came walking down the drive and got in beside Paul and accepted a cigarette.

"Vern, I know you're your own boy now. You're not on parole. You don't even have to listen to any advice I want to give you. You can get out and walk away and there's nothing I can do about it."

"I wouldn't do that, Mr. Darmond."

Paul sat so that he faced Vern. "What are you trying to do to Jana, Vern?"

Vern had been lifting his hand to take the cigarette from his lips. The hand stopped and was motionless for one long second. The lean handsome face became like a mask. "Just what is that supposed to mean? I don't get it."

"Don't try to kid me, Vern. Gus took you in. He's treated you right. It's a hell of a repayment for you to sleep with his wife."

Vern looked straight ahead for a long time. Then he looked at his cigarette. He said softly, "I guess maybe you're right, Mr. Darmond. I guess maybe it is a hell of a thing. What beats me is how you found out so fast."

"We won't talk about how I found out, boy."

"Honest, I tried to do the right thing, Mr. Darmond. But she sort of wore me down."

"How do you mean?"

"Oh, it's been going on for a long time. I don't mean I've been sleeping with her a long time. I mean she's been after me. When I work in the store she manages to work close to me. You know. Oh, I could tell what she wanted, all right, but I didn't want to do anything like that to Gus. I mean he's been swell to me. But you know how it is. He's pretty old, and Jana is full of Wheaties. I . . . sort of forgot myself finally. You know, if I stay around here, Mr. Darmond, I can't promise I'll stay away from her. I guess I'm . . . well, weak or something. Anyway, I'm not the only one getting it."

"What do you mean?"

"I'd rather not say."

"Would you be willing to leave, Vern?"

"The way I figure it, I've been here long enough. I ought to start thinking of bettering myself. Being more than a delivery boy. And I'm afraid there might be real trouble if Jana and I got caught. Sure, Mr. Darmond, I'm willing to leave."

"Do you want help locating another job?"

"No. I think I'll go somewhere else. Out west, maybe."

"When?"

Vern flicked the cigarette out the window. "I guess I could take off Sunday.

"Will that give Gus a chance to find another driver?"

"That new kid will work out O.K. Deliveries will be fouled up for a few days, but he'll catch on fast."

"Don't you think you ought to tell Gus you're planning to leave?"

"I'd rather not. Jana might make a stink about it. You know. Let something slip, or want to come with me or something."

"I think you're making good sense, Vern."

"Thanks, Mr. Darmond. I'm glad you talked to me like this. I can see now how I was headed for trouble. But you know how it is with a babe. You sort of forget yourself. It's time I took off."

"I think so too."

"Well, thanks for everything, Mr. Darmond. You've been swell to me. Really swell. I'll never forget you."

Paul returned the strong honest handclasp and looked into the too direct eyes. He sat and watched Lockter walk back up the drive, turn and wave and grin just before he went around the corner of the house. He sat for several minutes, vaguely unsatisfied with the talk. It had come out better than he had dared hope. It was like swinging hard at something and missing. He shrugged off his feeling of irritation and foreboding.

Bonny was standing in the shed passageway by the pile of crates of empty soft-drink bottles. Walter gave her an odd glance and as he started to go by her she said, "I want to talk to you."

"I got things to do."

"I want to talk to you right now, Walter."

"That sounds like you were trying to give orders around here. Let me tell you that when I'm ready for you to give me—"

"Don't bluster at me. I know you're taking money. And you know I know it. Stealing from your own father."

His eyes slid uneasily away from hers. "You crazy or something?" he asked sullenly.

"You can't bluff your way out of this, Walter."

"O.K. It's my money just as much as it is his. I'll take it if I feel like it."

"You aren't taking it. You're sneaking it out of the drawer. Altering receipts to make the cash-up balance. And I know why you're taking it."

He gave her a look of utter shock and surprise. "What!"

"You're taking it and hiding it away and when you have enough you're going to run like a miserable rabbit. All the states co-operate in returning husbands on the run. You'll be brought back. You know that, don't you?"

"I'll never come back here."

"How brave! How dramatic!"

"I can't take this much longer. I tell you I've taken it just as long as I can."

"If I were married to a mouse like you, Walter, I'd stick just as many pins in you as Doris does."

He frowned at her. "What do you mean?"

"I'd want to be married to a man. I'd want my man to be boss. I'd keep prodding at him to see just how much he'd take before turning on me and putting me in my place."

"Doris isn't like that."

"How do you know? Of course, you can't find out until after the baby comes. You can't start . . . disciplining her until after that."

"My God, you mean hit her? If I ever hit Doris she'd kill me."

"How do you know?"

"I just know."

"Aren't you bigger than she is?"

She watched him, watched the thought-masked face, the slow and curious straightening of the shoulders. She said quickly, "If I were a man I'd certainly at least try that before running like—"

"Like a rabbit," he said.

"Don't take any more money, Walter. I don't want it to be blamed on me. And if it were, I don't think you're man enough to clear me."

"I might take some more and I might not."

"Doris is sweet. You've turned her into a shrew by being so gutless."

"She was born a shrew."

"Was she? Then why did you marry her? Wasn't she different before she married you?"

"She fooled me."

"Or you fooled her, Walter. Lots of women who think they're marrying men are disappointed. Then they keep needling those men in the silly hope that somehow they'll begin to show some spirit."

"I got to think about this. I don't know. I think maybe you're wrong, Bonny. But honest, I never thought of anybody blaming you."

It was the psychological moment, so she turned and walked away from him, walked out into the store leaving him standing there with an expression in which trouble and vague hope were mixed. Her heart gave a high, hard, startling bound as she saw Paul standing tall near the cash register, chatting with Jimmy. He saw her and smiled toward her. She walked to him with a strange shy feeling.

"Lunch at the same place?" he asked.

She nodded.

Chapter Nineteen

THE EARLY-AFTERNOON SUN touched the gray stones. Bonny leaned against one and it dug into her back, but she did not mind. Paul's head was in her lap, the curve of the nape of his neck fitting perfectly her convex thigh. His eyes were shut and he was in the shadow of her. She traced her finger lightly along the upper lid of his eye and he shifted a bit and made a contented sound.

"Of all places, my darling," she said.

"Mmmm-hmmm."

"In fact, the worst possible place. Because of the other day. Didn't you know that?"

"You talk too much. Sure. Worst possible place. That's why I picked it."

He opened one eye and squinted up at her. "Mmm. Lovely colors. Blue sky, copper hair, gray eyes. Fine."

"As I said once before, my man, you make me feel so damn girlish."

"Technique. Make 'em all feel girlish. Lean over a bit farther. Like to see your hair swing out like that."

She bent down and with a movement of her head drew the sheaf of hair across his mouth and upper lip.

He caught her hand and kissed each finger in turn. "Want to hear a confession?"

"Make it exciting, and I'll listen."

"Sure. Very exciting. Darmond is a cold guy. Picked the time and the place. Coldly. A lab experiment. Says to himself: If it works, I marry the girl."

She felt very still. "Paul . . . I mean that's very nice. I'm flattered and so on. But . . . smart buyers don't want merchandise off the counter. They like it in the original wrappings. Hell, I mean this can go on as long as you like, and stop when you like. Isn't that enough?"

"If it works, I marry the girl. So it works. In fact, I distinctly remember every tree over in those woods falling over simultaneously, though now they seem to be miraculously upright." He looked up at her seriously. "It did work."

"There are no words, my darling. May I be coarse? Anything that happened from the waist down was purely coincidental. What mattered was having my heart break in a zillion pieces and go zooming out through the top of my head."

"It had to matter a lot—to you. You know why."

"Of course I know why. And it did, Paul. Can you believe that?"

"I can't believe otherwise."

"Thank you, darling," she said.

"Marriage, then. Sound institution."

"You better think that over, Paul. For quite a long time."

"O.K. Time me. Sixty seconds."

"Sixty days, at least."

He pursed his lips, then asked, "Would that actually make you feel better?"

"Yes. It would."

"And if at the end of sixty days I still like the idea?"

"Then we will go ahead with it, Paul. And if we go ahead with it, I swear—I swear, my darling, that I will be a good wife. And if you change your mind, I will be anything you want me to be."

He kissed her knuckles. "So be it."

"Far away," she said softly, "in a gloomy old world is a dismal market full of improbable people, and I should be there right now. But it doesn't seem to matter as much as it should. I love you, Paul."

"Oh, is that what it is? I love you, too."

He sat up then and stood up and gave her his hand and pulled her to her feet. They kissed and in the middle of the kiss lost their balance, staggered, laughed.

"Strong poison, my man," she said.

"Quick poison. Let's get out of here before you never get back to work."

As they drove back to the city she told him about not being able to sleep, about seeing Vern go to Jana after the truck had left. And he told her of his talk with Vern, and of the quite unexpected co-operation. And he told her of what Vern had implied, about someone else sharing Jana's favors.

"Paul, I can't quite believe that. Who would it be? Either Walter or Rick. Neither of them seems probable. Doris would scent something like that in a moment. And Rick Stussen seems so oddly unmasculine. Not a feminine type, just sort of—sexless."

"Does Gus go out early another day this week?"

"Saturday morning."

"Maybe Vern will see her then for the last time. And that time, the way fate usually handles these things, will be the time Gus forgets something and has to come back."

"Oh, no!"

"We'll just hope it works out all right. Hope he doesn't try to stretch his luck, as long as he's leaving Sunday anyway."

He pulled up to the curb and watched her quick long-legged stride as she went into the market. He knew at once that he did not want her there. He knew that he would get her away from there at the very first opportunity. It was not the place for her to be. Not the place for his woman to be.

Vern sat on the edge of his bed at ten o'clock on Friday night and once again went over all the steps that had been taken, and all the ones that would have to be taken. The timing was the most delicate problem. If it were timed right, it would go off right.

On Thursday night he had emptied the fruit jars into a small cardboard carton. While in the cellar he had put the hypo box into one of the holes where a fruit jar had been and he had tamped the dirt down firmly afterward. He had wrapped the cardboard carton in brown paper, tied it with stout string, taken it down to the railroad station, and put it in a coin locker. He wore a brown belt with a trick spring device to give it elasticity. He had shoved the locker key into the leather sleeve of the belt that concealed the spring. The device of the cardboard carton had a flexibility that pleased him. It could be taken along or mailed to a predetermined address.

Darmond's surprise accusation had rattled him badly. He hoped he had carried it off properly. It had become immediately necessary to find out how Darmond got the information. That had not been too difficult. He had caught Jana on the stairs an hour ago while the television was turned high.

She had not wanted to talk to him. He put one hand hard across her mouth and with the other he hurt her in a way he had been told about but had never tried before. It was alarmingly effective. When he released her, her face was the color of dirty soap and she could have fallen had he not grabbed her. Her color came back slowly. The threat of a second application made her willing to discuss the matter. It turned out that Bonny had gone to Jana, that something had made Bonny suspicious, and Jana, of course, had talked. So obviously Bonny had gone at once to Darmond.

The palms of his hands had begun to perspire. He rubbed them on a fresh handkerchief. At least the interview with Darmond had provided one advantage. It had given him a legitimate excuse, which Darmond would verify, for packing his belongings. The old suitcase, and the new one were in the closet, side by side. He saw himself checking them in at one of those hotels he had seen in the movies. Cabanas ringing the pool. Women deep-tanned and drowsy on the bright poolside mats. It would be one of the places where gambling was legal. He would hit a dozen of the gilded spots and then after a couple of weeks present himself at the nearest office of the Internal Revenue people and, acting earnest and confused, say, "Look, I don't want to get in any trouble, but I came out here looking for a job and I started gambling and I've made all this money and what do I do now?" They would take a large bit of it, but it would be worth it to give the cash a legitimate background, a reason for existence. Then, if a man was presentable and watched his step and had a little cash and dressed right, it wouldn't be too hard to move in on one of those moneyed dolls out there, because the gambling towns were divorce mills, and inevitably there would be one who was not only stacked, but also loaded, and rebounding high enough to catch on the fly. Vernon Karl Lockter will be joined in holy wedlock to Mrs. Delightful Gelt. Then let the organization try any squeeze plays. If you had the backings, you could always buy off pressure. And that piece of paper would be no damn good anyway. And then no nonsense about trying to inherit her money. It was much simpler just to take it away from her.

He shelved the bright dream and went downstairs. The ten-thirty program was just ending and the others had gone to bed and Gus sat woodenly, watching the bright screen. As the closing commercial came on, Gus got up and walked over and turned the set off and stood watching the scene collapse to a hard bright spot and then fade into blackness.

"Can I talk to you a minute, Gus?"

The old man turned, apparently becoming aware for the first time of another person in the room. "Talk? Go on. Talk."

"Not here, Gus."

"Where?"

"Come on, Pop. Outside. Walk around the block."

Gus stared at him and then shrugged and went with him. Vern walked beside him, and waited until they were a good hundred feet from the house.

"You've been swell to me, Gus. I appreciate it. I want to tell you something because . . . well, you've been swell to me, and I don't like to have something going on without you knowing about it."

Gus stopped with a street light slanting across his heavy face, emphasizing the brutal lines, erasing the kindliness.

"Talk plain, Vern."

"I will. You know when you go out early in the morning and go to the farmers' market?"

"Yes, yes. I know. Talk."

"Well, when you leave, right after you leave, somebody sneaks into bed with your wife. Understand, I don't know who it is."

Gus did not move or speak. Vern thought perhaps the old guy hadn't understood. He said, "Did you hear me?"

Gus made a low sound in his throat and turned back toward the house. Vern grabbed his wrist and said, "Wait a minute, Pop. Hold up a minute."

Gus yanked his arm free with surprising strength. Vern trotted by him and turned and blocked the way, saying, "Wait!"

He had to walk backward, avoiding repeated attempts to thrust him out of the way until at last the old man stopped. "Wait for what? She do that to me? With these hands I—"

"No Pop. Don't you get it? You got to find out who the guy is."

"I beat it out of her."

"That's no good. Understand, I don't have any proof."

"Then how you know?"

"I got up early Thursday. I was going down the stairs and I looked down the hall and I saw somebody coming out of her room. A man. He saw me and dodged back in. It was too dark to see who it was. What good will it do if she denies everything? You got to catch them, Gus. That's the best way."

"How?"

"You don't say anything, see? Tomorrow morning you get up at four, like always. I'll wake up the kid when I go back and tell him not to wait downstairs for you in the morning. To go ahead and take the truck and drive it to that all-night gas station and fill it up and bring it back and you'll be waiting. Then you don't go downstairs. What you do is go *up*stairs. Just to the landing. We'll wait there and see if anybody comes. See? Then you got the proof."

"My Jana. I cannot think she—Ah, my God, the trouble! All trouble. Everything. Henry. My Teena. Jana. Ah, my God!"

"Do it my way, Gus."

After a long time the man nodded. "Your way, then."

After they went back Vern stood nervously on the stairs near the second-floor landing, listening for sounds of violence. The house was still. When he was certain that the old man would do it his way, he knew that the most ticklish part of it was done.

He went quietly down and through the house and went into Rick's room without knocking and turned on the light. Rick sat bolt upright, squinting, his mouth open with surprise.

"What's the matter, Vern? What's the matter?"

Vern sat on the foot of the bed and said in a low tone, "Relax, dearie. Nothing's wrong." He lit a cigarette and gave Rick a crooked smile. "Guilty conscience or something?"

"What do you want, waking me up?"

"You got an alarm clock?"

Rick pointed to it. "Sure."

"Gus wants you to go along with him in the morning. Something about picking up a big meat order. Here, I'll set it for four. He wants you to get up and go up and wake him up. Got that?"

"Sure."

"Don't knock and don't turn on any lights. Just go on in there quiet like a mouse and shake him."

"O.K."

"I told him I'd give you the word." Vern got up and went to the door and turned and said. "Don't let it bother you if you hear the truck drive out, Rick. I heard him telling the kid to take it over and gas it up and bring it back to pick up you two."

He turned off the light and closed the door behind him. He felt excited, tensed up, very alive. He went quietly out through the kitchen and the shed and into the store. He drifted by the shadowy racks and went behind the meat case and took hold of the hard greasy handle of the meat cleaver and wrested the blade out of the chopping block. He hefted it for a moment in his hand, and then unbuttoned the bottom button of his shirt and put the cleaver inside, its blade resting chill against his skin.

It was at that moment that he had a sudden doubt. In spite of all the careful planning, he realized he had made one very stupid and obvious mistake. There had been absolutely no need to have anything to do with Jana. It could have been worked in precisely the same way without even touching her. And that would have removed certain elements of risk. Suppose the old man didn't kill her. She could chatter and the old man could chatter, and that goddamn Rowell could add the two stories together and come up with a bad answer. If he'd never touched her, she wouldn't be able to do anything but deny having anything to do with Stussen. And with the old man finding Stussen in his bedroom, her story would look sick. He wondered why he had made such an obvious mistake. He stood silently until the doubt began to fade. The old man would be as insane as you could make anyone. And it was pretty damn certain that he wouldn't leave anything alive in the room.

He went back and up the stairs and hid the cleaver in his room and woke up the kid and told him to take the truck over and gas it up and bring it back to pick up the old man in the morning. He gave the kid a five-dollar bill for the gas. When he got back in his room it was a quarter after twelve. He turned out the table lamp and sat on the bed in the darkness. He knew he wouldn't sleep. Not when there was so little time left.

Chapter Twenty

PAUL DARMOND lay in darkness, his fingers laced at the back of his neck. He turned and looked at the clock. The luminous hands made the right angle of three o'clock. He remembered the tall good look of her as she walked away from him. He did not believe in premonition, but he had slept several times, and had awakened each time with the nagging thought that he would never see her again. That forever in his mind would be that last look of her as she walked away.

The clock said ten after three.

He sat up in the darkness and threw the covers aside and sat on the edge of the bed. He yawned and dressed slowly in the darkness. He let himself out and stood in front of the building. It was three-thirty. He turned resolutely in the opposite direction from the market and the old shambling house. He walked a few blocks and then slowed and stopped and stood for a time, and turned back and walked slowly back and passed his apartment. It was childish, but he knew it would make him feel better to just walk by the place where she slept. He wished he knew which window was hers.

When he was two blocks from the house he quickened his step, and felt an odd prickling of apprehension at the nape of his neck.

But when he arrived at the house it stood huge and dark and silent. He stood in the soft warm night on the narrow sidewalk looking up at the third-floor windows. Like, he thought, a lovesick kid.

The second-floor light startled him when it went on. Then he realized it was probably Gus getting up to go down to the market.

The sound came loudly, shocking its way through **him**. It was like no sound he had ever heard before. It took him the space of three heartbeats to identify it for what

164

it was: the hard full crazy-throated screaming of a woman, short shrill bursts of screaming as she sucked her breath in, let it burst out in a scream lasting no more than a second, and then did it again and again. He ran for the front door of the house as hard as he could run, and as he went up the steps in one bound, the last metronomic scream was abruptly cut off. He tore the door open and ran up the flight of stairs.

Filled with the restlessness of a sense of impending trouble, Lieutenant Rowell, after the last of the joints in his area had closed, cruised slowly down the empty streets, making random turns. The metallic voice suddenly filled the car. Rowell listened, and then made a U turn, bouncing the right front wheels off the far curb, and tromped the gas pedal down hard. He shrieked to a stop in front of the Varaki house and drew his short muzzled revolver as he went toward the front porch in a bandy-legged run.

Rick woke up when the alarm went off. He was astonished to see that it was dark outside. It took him a few moments to remember why he had got up at this hour. He felt sodden and greasy with sleep. He turned on the light and dressed quickly. He felt abused. Saturday was always a hard day. Now people wanted you to get up before the birds did.

He went quietly through the house and tiptoed up the stairs to the second floor. He started down the hall and thought he heard a sound behind him, a sort of grunting and a stir of movement. He stopped and listened and heard no other sound. Darkness had always made him uncomfortable, had always given him the feeling of something all teeth that was about to jump out at him. He licked his lips. He stopped in front of Gus's door and he wanted to knock at the door. Behind the door was a bed where a man and a woman slept together. He did not like to think about that. He wiped his hand on the side of his pants and gingerly turned the knob and opened the door. He wanted to cough or something. He tiptoed in and he could make out the bed. He could barely see the prone figure of the sleeper. As he tiptoed across the room he could hear breathing sounds. It didn't sound just right for somebody sleeping because they seemed too fast. He stood by the bed, peering down, and wiped his hand on the side of his pants again and reached gingerly down to shake Gus by the shoulder. His hand brushed and touched an odd heavy roundness, and something caught at his sleeve. He heard a hard thumping like somebody running. Somebody running in the hall. And the harsh overhead light went on suddenly and there alone in the bed was Jana, and he turned quickly toward the door and saw a man running at him, mouth wide open and twisted in a funny way, a man with a face he didn't know for a moment, and then he saw it was Gus running toward him. He felt his own lips stretch in the smile that had protected him from so many things, and he said, "I was just—" And he saw Vern in the doorway behind Gus and felt relief because Vern would explain. And he saw a flashing glint in the light and saw in a thunderous part of a second what Gus was doing to him even as the quick flashing slanted up toward his head, and the flashing turned into a great hard white hot burning light that slid him tumbling over in brightness like a bug in a lamp shade, tumbling, grinning, his ears saying back to him "just . . . just . . . just . . ." in the instant before a great hairy hand turned out all the lights in the world.

He had squatted on the stairs with Vern and he heard the slow creaking as some animal that walked on two legs like a man began to make his cautious way up the stairs. Violator of my house and my pride and my dignity as a man. Someone who waited until the little truck rattled away and who thinks now he is safe from the vengeance of the Lord God Almighty.

And he comes closer and turns down my hall toward my wife, filled with his animal lust, and I cannot keep entirely quiet. I make a small noise and someone near me I have forgotten in this moment puts his hand on my mouth. Then I am still and the one who creeps toward my wife stops and we wait and listen for a sound of each other like animals in the forest darkness. I am still and he walks on and then the one with me fumbles at my hand and my fingers close around the good and familiar handle of the great cleaver, the one kept razor-keen by Rick. It feels good in my hand and by now the animal has had time to reach my wife. I start quietly down, and

I am quiet until I reach the hall and then I can be quiet no longer. I run and reach around the doorframe and snap on the light and half blinded I see her eyes and the man who turns is Rick, and as I run at him I swing the good keen weight, swinging it up with all strength and hate, and feel the good deep bite and hear the deep wet sound of the way it bites up into the animal brain of the thing I kept in my house and never knew. And I wrench the blade free as he is falling, his pink hands half lifting as he falls. And her mouth is wide and the cords in her throat stand out and she is sitting, kicking her way back away from me. And I take one step and there is a funny breaking in my chest, with something warm that spreads itself inside there. I am on my knees and the house had tilted so that the floor is a hill that slopes to the window. And I go over face down on the hill slope feeling the warm wetness inside my chest and wondering about it, and at the same time watching the slow rug pattern come up, and come close to my face and strike hard against my cheek, yet without pain. And as I am wondering curiously about these things, the slope becomes steeper and it is very slippery, and I slide down the slope to the dark window and through it and fall down out of the dark window, turning in the air in darkness and thinking that this is something of a great oddness indeed . . .

He crouched beside Gus on the stairs and together they listened to the silence, and then to the slow creaking as Rick continued on down the hall. He had his hand on Gus's shoulder and felt the movement of the shoulder muscles. He found Gus's hand in the darkness and worked the cleaver handle into it and let go cautiously as he felt the shift of weight. He gave a gentle push at the broad old back. The old man went quietly down the stairs, but as he reached the hallway with Vern close behind him, he began to run. Vern ran quickly after him. He saw the room lights shine out into the hall the instant the old man ran through the doorway. Vern stopped in the doorway. He saw the hard swing, matched to the plunging run, and saw Rick's smile and the soft uplifting of the small hands as the blade hit just under his left ear, upslanting, cutting jaw, brain, and smile. Jana screamed the first time as Rick fell, and she scuttled backward away from the approaching menace of the cleaver.

She screamed again and Gus faltered and dropped heavily to his knees, shaking the room, as though the very scream itself had knocked him down. He saw what he had to do quickly and he scampered frantically for the cleaver, snatching it off the floor near the still hand of Gus. She sat back in the corner, eyes squeezed tight shut, chin up, throat taut with the constant nerve-shattering screams. He swung hastily at her but the cleaver tip bit into the wall and the blade stopped an inch from her temple. He wrenched it out and as she began another scream he struck again at the source of the scream, knowing only that he had to make that sound stop.

The sound of the truck driving out awakened Bonny. She thought perhaps it would help Jana if she were to open her door if Vern started out of his room to go down to her. She put on her robe and stood close to her door, listening for any sound. For a long time there was no sound. At last she thought she heard somebody moving about on the floor below. She cautiously opened her door in order to be able to listen a bit better. The slow seconds went by. And then she heard somebody running along the hall below her.

There was then a sound that seemed to come up through the floor. A hard scream of ultimate terror. There was a sound of something heavy falling. Her scalp prickled all over as the scream came quickly on the heels of the last one. Without conscious awareness of how she got there, she found herself at the head of the stairs as the screams kept coming. When she was midway down the stairs the screams stopped and there was a more terrible silence. She hurried down the hall to the patch of light shining through the door. Walter came out into the hall in pajamas too big for him, staring stupidly.

As she reached the doorway she heard the odd sound. She looked into the room. She saw the split melon that had been Rick Stussen's head. She saw Gus, face down. She saw the man who knelt on the bed. He held a red cleaver in both hands. He struck with solemn intentness, like a small boy hammering nails. For a moment her mind could not encompass the enormity of what she was looking at. She stood and frowned and in the moment of his turning to look at her she was able to focus her mind on what the eyes had already seen. The room turned vague and she swayed sideways against the door-frame.

She would have fainted, she knew, had he not turned and looked at her. He wore a dead face. From the eyes down, the face was utterly, hideously slack, as though all the muscles of cheeks and mouth had been removed. The slack face seemed to hang from the eyes. And the eyes were utterly dull, absorbing all light and reflecting none. And as he started toward her, smeared, stained, hideous out of the charnel stink of the room, she turned and ran for the stairway, wanting only to get out into the night, to run down the dark street.

She blundered hard into Paul Darmond, hearing behind her the bang of the door as Walter popped back into his room. She clawed at Paul as he tried to hold her, and she yelled, "Run! Oh, run!"

His dullness of wit in that moment infuriated her. She heard the familiar clattering sound of the truck coming into the drive and, out front, a hard screech of tires as a car stopped quickly. She knew that she could not bear to scramble past Paul and leave him to face what came down the hallway. Perhaps only a moment passed before he sensed and comprehended the immediacy of the danger. His fingers locked hard on her wrist and they went down the stairs and she could hear it coming after them. It was like one of the nightmare of childhood, like running through glue, your steps a slow drifting, while something comes after, comes nearer.

They went out the front door and across the porch and down the front steps, and Rowell, with the gun in his hand, was one of the most comforting things she had ever seen.

"What is it?" he demanded, his voice unexcited.

"Vern," she said. "He's killing them."

Rowell went across the porch and into the dark house. Paul said, "Wait in his car, Bonny."

"No. You can't do anything. There's nothing you can do. Don't go back in there." She was beginning to shake all over, her teeth chattering, wavering as she stood. He put his arm strong abound her shoulders. There were lights on in most of the houses. People had come out on porches in robes and coats.

Another police car came riding in on the siren's wail

and two uniformed men piled out and trotted heavily toward the house and the sound that came out of the open front door stopped them in their tracks. A chittering whinnying sound, a sound of pure madness.

There was a thrashing and a scrambling and silence. The porch light came on and the hall light came on. Rowell appeared in the doorway, his face cramped with pain, nursing his right hand against his stomach.

His voice was ancient and rusty with pain, yet full of authority. "Moran. Get out there and call in. There's some deads upstairs and a crazy in the hall and I need a doc. I got a busted hand. Bracelet that crazy while he's still out, Schantz. Wrists *and* ankles. There's a kid sitting on him."

Inside the house a woman began to scream. It was not like the other screaming. This was thin, weak, perulant. One cop had trotted out to the prowl car. The other had gone in the house. Walter came hurrying out onto the porch. "The baby's coming!" he hollered. "The baby's coming!" Sirens grew in the distance. "Do something, somebody!" Walter yelled.

The intern on the first ambulance, at Rowell's request, gave his attention first to Doris Varaki. She was sent off in the family sedan, Walter driving.

Paul said to Bonny, "You can't stay here. I'll have one of the police sedans drive us to my place."

"I'm all right. I'll be all right."

Rowell said, quite softly, as though explaining to himself, "Not a sound when I went in there. Not a damn sound. Some light coming down the stairs. Then something moves right beside me and as I start to turn around he chops at my hand, chops at the gun with that cleaver. Didn't know what it was then. Thought it was a club. Handle must have been slippery and turned in his hand, because he broke my hand with the flat of it. Had me trapped then, right against the wall at the foot of the stairs. Saw what he was holding. Saw that face. My God! Never closer to dying. Couldn't even twitch. Then that punk came out of nowhere. Came in through the back someplace. That pet of yours, Preach. One of those gutless wonders of yours. Oh, damn him! Saw everything in a split second and banged into Lockter so the swing of that cleaver missed my face by a half a whisker. And Lockter turned around and the punk ducked the swing and grabbed him. I came out of the trance and yanked that cleaver away from him. Then the crazy started making those gobbling noises and going for the kid's eyes with his hands. That punk kid, Paul, he shoved him away and chopped him one right on the button. Oh, God, a pretty punch."

"That punk kid," Paul said softly.

Rowell looked up at them. "I know. I know. What am I going to do?"

"Thank him, I'd imagine."

"Back up, you people!" Moran bellowed. "Nothing to see. Nothing to see here. Back up. Break it up!"

As It Was in the Beginning

THERE IS A STONE city and in it a gray neighborhood, and in the neighborhood there is a small market, a cement block structure with an umbilical shed attaching it to a large shabby house.

Trade is fairly good these days. People who traded there before the bloody maniacal mess on that soft June night say that all Walter needed to turn him into a man was the sudden hard burden of responsibility. Doris works in the store. She has grown considerably more plump, but that is not unbecoming. She has a sharp tongue, but Walter is able to quiet her infrequent tantrums with a single look or a word. Anna looks after the child, a boy who is just learning to walk, and the more eagle-eyed customers predict another.

There is a new butcher, a quiet, soft-eyed man, but he is not as good as Stussen was. James Dover does a lot of the buying and handles all deliveries and manages also to attend adult-education courses three nights a week at the university. The heavy schedule has leaned him and matured him. He and Teena had no time for a honeymoon. There was talk, of course in the neighborhood, but there would have been more if that hideous night in June had not provided a more drastic subject. But talk falters and dies and time changes things, and in one year a good true thing can be built on marshy ground. Rumor and suspicion dilute the few known facts until at last there is a mere residue of vaguest doubt that can be washed out of the mind of him who chances to see the look in a young bride's eyes as she looks at the clean strength of her young husband.

As the papers in the newspaper files slowly yellow, the facts are forgotten. A few people remember the fourteen-hour tape recording made from the babblings of the crazy man. One hour of useful information was edited out of that tape. The information had no legal status, of course. Yet it was used to hound those mentioned in the tape until Karshner himself, in an almost apoplectic rage, quite suddenly died. Certain newspaper correspondents pointed out the wry fact that death came from the bursting of the same great artery that had burst in the thick chest of Gus Varaki.

Certain tentacles of the Johnston wholesale-retail drug organization were chopped off, and the organization suffered a temporary inconvenience. Yet the head of the beast was not touched, and in time new tentacles have grown, extending themselves cautiously through the dark places of the city. New children are learning how to float. Folded packets of hand-hot money are passed in the lobbies of the cheapest movie houses, in alleys, in the men's rooms of cheap bars, in the candy stores near the high school. It goes on because as yet the rewards are greater than the risk for the conscienceless.

Perhaps, as Bonny believes, for people in the jungle of the city it is a matter of luck. Luck with, as Paul insists, a bit of faith, too. Not a specific faith. Just an ability to believe in something. Luck seems to have come back to the high-shouldered old house and the oblong fluorescence of the market.

Bonny and Paul went there last night at closing time for a reaffirmation of their own faith, their own luck. They are together, and they are married, and they are not as yet happy, though they hope to be. They swing between high peaks of great joy in each other, swing through the valleys of bitterness, of trying to hurt each other. They had to come across the city because they rent one of the faculty houses at the university and hope to furnish it properly with the money from the consultant work Paul is doing outside the classroom. They are not yet sure, either of them, that this marriage will work, yet they are trying to make it work.

They went to the market at closing time and after the door was locked Jim opened some cans of cold beer and the six of them talked for a time. They talked of small things and they laughed together in a good way. At one point Doris brought tension into the place by speaking bitterly of the money that was found in the coin locker with the one clear fingerprint that was identified as Lockter's, and the impounding of that money,

and how it ought to have been turned over to what was
left of the Varaki family. Lockter, incurably paranoid,
would certainly never see any of it, or see anything beyond the walls of that place where he is kept until the
day when he will die, a crazed old man of many visions.
But Walter gave her a short harsh look and she returned
it for one antagonistic moment before her eyes softened
and she smiled at some private secret and began quickly,
almost apologetically, to speak of other things.

When Paul and Bonny left they walked hand in hand
to the old car, in a rare moment of peace and accord.
She sat close to him as they drove across the city, through
the neon wasteland, through the stone jungle, holding
close this small warm time of luck and of faith.

Number 12 in the bestselling Travis McGee series by

JOHN D. MacDONALD

THE LONG LAVENDER LOOK

It began the way all McGee's adventures began. From left field. Only this time it was right in front of his car.

This lovely young thing, wearing little more than a frightened look, streaked out of darkness into his headlights. McGee hit the brakes, missed the nymphet's tawny haunch by one micro-second, and landed upside down in ten feet of swamp water.

Two minutes later, with McGee upright and limping along the deserted Florida road, someone zoomed by in an old truck and took a couple of shots at him. McGee went to the local sheriff to complain—and found himself arrested for murder . . . .

X3548   **$1.75**